"Chocs away"
papers arrived yet
Fawlty!

Titus Unlive

by

~~Colin Sloan~~

Colin Sloan

First Published in Great Britain in 2011 by

Resurgam Press

The Lock Keepers House

26 Ballyskeagh Road, Lisburn, BT27 5TE

ISBN 978-0-9567948-0-2

A catalogue record for this book is available
from the British Library

Typeset in Adobe Garamond Pro

Cover design and layout by KFN

Cover illustration © Andrew Haslett, 2010

Printed in Great Britain by

MPG Biddles Limited

24 Rollesby Road, Norfolk

For Brendan Murphy

Dear Sirs,

RE: HB19 09 003, 13 Joys Entry

We would like to draw your attention to the fact that your proposed demolition of the property would be contrary to policy BH8 of the Department's Planning Policy Statement 6: Planning Archaeology and the Built Heritage in that the building is listed under Article 42 of the Planning (NI) Order 1991.

We urge your client to take note of this listing, and ensure that remedial steps are taken to ensure the dwellings status.

Yours Faithfully,

Verily Blandon
Historic Buildings Unit

1

I just love the tone of this! Verily is as detached and as draughty as the properties she defends. She is the fulcrum of a hub of architectural snobbery trying to play catch up with the sorry list of neglected buildings they let slip since the 1960's. Any Commercial and domestic applications from replacement dwellings to ripping out the regency thunder box and all those in-between, fall within her remit. Verily stands between me and the closure of a lucrative deal on a parcel of land within the Cromac Ward of Belfast. My American clients, with whom I have building up a rapport for the last two years, will have to accede to her demands, however reluctantly and the development will have to consume the existing dwelling as it stands, affecting any design outcome. In frustration at this, I lift my Macy's snow globe and give it a thorough shaking, before twisting its key and instantly regretting it as the trill refrains of 'Blue Ridge Mountains Of Virginia' circulate around the office. Luckily, it's near 5.30 and we don't have many clients, except a downsizing widow and an aspirational couple, picking out property portfolios beyond their budget. Gordon, my boss, pops his head out of his office and looks at me in the manner of Oliver Hardy. I can see his point, I'm no greenhorn, but as I can no longer light up at my desk, then throttling the snow globe seemed the next best thing. I will have to contact the site developer, Mylagan & Love and let them know. Maybe they can make an offer to the owner, so they can enclose the property in some way. Anyway that's tomorrow, I can see Sarah and Gilchrist chomping at the bit to down tools, a daily indicator of what the time is. Poor Sarah! Always the same, the rush for the bus to Carryduff, tv dinners and dog food, the loneliness of a long distance Springer Spaniel praying on her mind as she mounts the Four Winds. I can't remember Sarah in a relationship, yet on the few occasions she is asked out for an after work drink, she always makes some excuse like her Spaniel needs clipping, or her father is coming over for dinner. Gilchrist is a jock, plays squash after work in another direction, he drives a Mazda MX 5, which has had its stereo nicked twice in the street he lives in. His court bookings are always shaved in half by traffic delays, making him tetchy with Graham, his opponent. So he often wins not by skill, but angered frustration. Gilchrist is a 'Hitter', part of that front line sales team eager for any tender morsels to endear themselves to the holders of the keys of the corporate motorcade. I, on the other hand, drive an early nineties Cincque Cinqco, a legacy from my first wife, a memento which I still can't afford to trade in. I have never had my stereo stolen, which gives me a grain of satisfaction as I try to upgrade my affections for this Italian classic!

Slowly the office clears, newbies give up trying to impress and collect their coats, office cliques form a pupae and turn into drinking buddies, sales conversion becomes exaggerated in theme pub booths, where every round of WKD stems the body's natural desires to eat. Bonds are formed here, sales teams learn rivalry and horseplay, stumbling into office relationships with the certainty of a sleepwalker.

This may sound rich, but it's true now as it ever was, the labelling has moved on, hairstyles change and instant messaging kills any mystery, but I was part of this; the first with the most, the last to leave. The partners instil this in us, they groom it, the competitive edge, they want young, raw, burnable talent and they want it in constant supply.

This is the inevitable axiom, age catches up with guile, I caught a glimpse of myself in a pub mirror five years ago, and I didn't like what I saw and left. The 'Hitters' are welcome to it, I like to think that I am a bit of a sage who knew when to back off, sure I'm still in the game, but I have specialised, moved on, I can offer advice, not that they will ever ask for any. But it's there if they want it, seasoned wood behind the new plantings, halfway up the Lisburn Road for the better part of 21 years.

As usual I'm the last but one to leave, locking Gordon in behind me. After an interminable delay, which could only happen here, due to country types insisting on taking their manicured cattle to the busy thoroughfares of Belfast, otherwise known as the Balmoral Show, I finally get home. Gemma has beaten me to the punch and the hot water. She has a leaving do to attend and is shaving her legs with my razor. I don't mind as long as I get to watch, I don't begrudge her frugal nature, when it is wrapped up in such an alluring package. How long has it been now? Better not ask, she's still got it, stepping in and out of dresses, a Vettriano muse in stay-up stockings. She knows damn well what this does to me, I really need a shower.

'There's some cold cuts in the fridge or pasta salad,' she says.

'Where are you all meeting up?' I ask.

'Cafe Xtrablatt, you know that place Franklin revamped, used to be Mahoney's.'

She's ready and says she will get a taxi home and blows a kiss through the steam in the bathroom mirror before leaving. I forget to get a towel and dry off with the one she used earlier. I open a window slightly and the room begins to clear. I take out a pair of tweezers and pluck out the strays in my eyebrows and nostrils. This regimen is in answer to the fact that I now grow hair where I need it least and lose it where I need it most. I balance one foot, then the other on the toilet seat and cut toenails into the bowl with consummate skill. Finally I grab a wedge of loo roll and dampen it under the tap before wiping up any errant hairs or filings from the bathroom floor. Nice!

I wonder what I did with all that free time I had before necessary grooming kicked in. I didn't consider henna hair mudpacks excessive, or the cultivation of gel dried stems into corn stocks unnatural back in the day. It was more of a ritual badge you wore, big hair was expected, the mark of the clan you aspired to; Goth, neurotic outsider, mod, romantic, new wave or post-punk. Who gave the order to pull the trigger that wound in my hairline? Does the hair we lose down the plughole make its way to the open sea and form a reef? Or does it settle at the bottom to form drifting shanks in the tide? Why do my ears keep growing? Could these folds on my face hold banknotes? When did my chin become so intimate with my neckline? Where have these concerto lines on my forehead come from? Answers on a postcard please.

I will raid the fridge for leftovers and content myself that the future looks brighter through the bottom of a glass. There's nothing on that I want to watch, so I can doze a bit on the sofa with the sound down. You ever get that feeling like you did before you went under anaesthetic?

Like you were about to disappear beneath your ribs while you are deaf to those around you. This is happening to me, and it's not like I'm overtired or something. Maybe I should have had another drink to help me relax more, but the position I'm in does it for me and soon I'm under.

Without looking, he grabs my hand, his cold palm, his innate strength. He leads me half way down an entry, roughly parallel with the Morning Star. His coat has seen better days, many days by the look of it, pinching him at the shoulders, with a high collar that's out of any fashion.

'What's the hurry?' I hear myself shout as he splashes me again on the puddled flag stones. He loosens his grip in a doorway, peeling fly posters at right angles fused with urine. I must have passed here a thousand times without ever noticing, he turns the key in the lock with some degree of difficulty. He was vulnerable there for a moment, with his back to me, crooked in this light, but my legs feel drunk and it's all I can do to stand here and watch him. He turns to face me for the first time, an elusive smile with just a hint of menace.

'This must all seem a little confusing for you?'
I cannot reply.
'Please enter of your own free will and leave some of your warmth behind.'
I swear it was said without a trace of irony.
'Titus Unlive at your service, Sir.'

He's completely thrown me with the theatrics, he grabs my hand again, shakes it vigorously in the speckled rays of the door fanlight. My eyes adjust to his stare, which although unsettling, lead me to relax my guard a bit. He leads me through the waxen glow of a half panelled hallway to the kitchen area.

'Good, shall we sit?'
Two Windsor chairs settle either side of the grate, overhung by a kettle swing. The fire is still glowing as the ash reaches the edge of the hearth. The window in the room is single glazed with an empty birdcage hanging

at its centre, the ledge is peeling and covered in clay pipes and broken crockery.

'Please excuse the mess, I have so very few visitors, it hardly seems worthwhile to make an effort.'

'What is happening to me? I am dreaming you...this is too real.'

'I know, that's not uncommon at first. You are sleeping, but you are awake to me, I have presented myself to you, you have followed me here, albeit I took your hand and led you. You are conscious of me and yet in your reality, your body is sub-conscious.'

He rises and walks to a dresser in an arched recess by the chimneybreast. He decants what must be wine into two pewter cups.

'Will you join me in some sack?'

I reach for the cup with a fixed gaze, taking in every portion of his demeanour. His age is hard to discern, unkempt hair falls foul of any style, his skin is pale, but there is vibrancy about him that I could feel within his grip. His eyes are too dark in this room for me to agree on a colour.

'Please join me in a toast to friendship,' he says. His countenance looks sincere as he raises his cup.

'To friendship,' I hear myself say weakly.

A nervous gulp from a sharp edged pewter cup follows. Without an interval, I take a second to salve any parched nerves. This wine he called 'sack' is excellent, it soothes the nerves in my face, warming my complexion involuntarily. I find myself sinking into the chair, resting my arms towards the firelight.

'Good,' he says. 'It was all I could do to stop your mind racing.'

We sit across from each other, I don't want to stare, so I ask about the painting behind him in the other recess beside the fire.

'I'm glad you asked, it is a relation, he was an émigré who had a workshop in this building.'

A relation?...this fella is wearing a wig, like a judge or King Billy! I want to ask more, the buttons on my shirt pop open, I can feel the stroke of her nails.

'Gemma!'

'You looked so vulnerable lying there.'

'What time is it?'

'Just gone 12, let me give you a nightcap.'

She has a leather jacket on just above her waist, she sits astride me on the couch, sweeping her hair across my face. I can smell the night air mixed with cigarettes. She giggles as I peel her apart, awake to her attentions.

'Did you have a good night?' I ask.

'I am now.'

'You could have saved me a lot of bother if you had done this earlier.'

I run my hands slowly across her skirt, she leans over me and we begin. Funny thing that, I slept like a log all night, no dreams or visitations, curled up behind her listening to her breathing, sending me off, until the birds began. I'll tell her about my dream later, after a drink, when she won't laugh so hard and dismiss me out of hand. I stroke her back. It's a bit plaintive, but if she's in the mood, she turns to face me and opens one eye and then down periscope beneath the duvet. The slit in the shutters guides me to the door, I creep off and have a wash and a pee. Brushing my teeth, looking out over the rooftops and the fields beyond, I mull over what happened. What exactly did happen? You dreamt about some creepy guy, you even went into his house and had a drink with him. And all this before you even went to bed. Bizarre or what? At least it felt like you did, I swear I could still taste the wine before I washed my teeth. Wise up! You dreamt it! Endof! God I hate that expression. Why did I use it then? It, along with the catalogue of other insincere terms like, 'nat a problem', 'thanking you', 'at the end of the day' and most annoyingly, 'across the water'. Smite me now, they are out of the way.

I tune into Nostalgia FM on the way to work, half way through a lesser-known Associates single called 'Gloomy Monday'. Me and a handful of other men of a certain age, stuck at the lights, tapping on the wheel, oblivious to how sad we look.

The spurious e-mails have piled up, I siphon them, one catches my eye though, a leggy blonde from this years crop sits on a desk draped in little else but my old school blazer. I look at the sender address, Successonaplate.com, that'll be Rawnsley! Hugo to his mates, of which I am a tenuous one. Hugo didn't bother his arse at school, his diffident air was infectious and I walked out of numerous exams to be part of his clique. His email address sums him up better than I ever could, the confidence that I never had, just poured out of him. Here's me thinking that some of that would rub off on me, some chance! Hugo was one of the few in my year who had their own car, yes I know it's commonplace now, but turning up in the quad in an open top before assembly was pretty cool. He was on the Sixth Form Committee and played for the 1st XV, his easy charm meant he always had a girl and a plausible excuse for any teacher.

'Hiya Bones,' my nickname at school, not a good start.

'You still working for those saddo's at Biggin Hill?' This is encrypted speak for 'loser'.

'Just wanted to remind you that I am organising the class reunion this year, November 28th at the Reform Club. Bit near Crimbo, but hope you can make it. We can have posh nosh, then a tour of the City after dark with some foreign Jonny! Anyway send my love to Emma, Hugo.'

It's Gemma! How many times do I have to tell him? It wouldn't phase him in the slightest, he would brush off any faux pas so easily, he never embraced correctness and it didn't seem to do his career any harm. I will have to get back to him, he has given plenty of notice and he does mean well. Anyway it would be good to catch up, I will make a point of calling into his restaurant, 'La Stanza', some evening on the way back from work. It must be twenty-five years since we both left Cropredy. My God, where did the time go? Hugo for all his faults, never really left. He was there for a good time, not an academic one, in the back of his mind he knew that he could cook and charm, so he networked, kept in touch, put his face about and found his niche. I can't fault him for that, he was so bloody popular, but he always seemed interested in what you were doing and not in a selfish way. He went abroad, did his apprenticeship, married into money and opened a restaurant. Anyway, he was right. I still work for those Boffins at Biggin Hill! They wasted a lot of time and finance on finding a new name for a role I have been doing with moderate success. The salary reflects my lack of ambition. I can get by on it without giving in to change. Somehow, and don't ask me how, I have managed to avoid the numerous culls and take-overs that I have witnessed over the last 21 years. At the last guess we are currently a subsidiary of Lydon & Dye Property Consultants and Auctioneers, but this is subject to change, and probably will. As I try to perfect the art of bending in the wind, ducking those intermittent requests to comply with contract harmonisation, I can afford to wax a little on how this once was a good business. Well, actually, I can't, because it never was, only now the gloves are definitely off and the knuckles are bare.

Mr Retchett, a man who I never worked for, used a small inheritance to buy up bombsites just after the war. He cleared these brown field sites and put up temporary accommodation in the form of Nissan huts and prefab homes. The thing is I can remember these 'temporary homes' in the late 1970's, he squeezed as many as he could onto a site until they became known as 'Tin Towns'. With the monies gathered in rent, he set up a property business which had built up a considerable portfolio right across deprived areas of Belfast. Mr Retchett at 89 would still put in two working days a week, taking pride in the ability to lift heavy files from his car boot, prospective properties to be drooled over and logged on to his computer in the back office. He died the year I joined, so I witnessed his son redecorate and remodel the office, out went the panelling and bankers lamps, in came the Hessian wallpaper and low-level lighting. It was a revamp, but the period charm worked well on older clients and was now lost, some details should have been kept in such an old building, but it was as if the son was trying to obliterate his memory, his widow never came back after collecting his personal stuff. Young Mr Retchett, he was never called that of course, too Dickensian, would also put in a two-day week, but at the wrong side of 45, he was more interested in the secretarial hosiery and the calibre of his golfing equipment. Fortunately we had Gordon, who would burn the midnight oil to such an extent that I would receive calls to key holders from the Police on a regular basis regarding our half open shutter door. Gordon is like an 'Old Retainer', married to the job, and as such has proved his worth, it was only a matter of time before Toby Retchett took advantage of him and decided to cash in. The office dynamics were simple, a glass brick wall the length of the building on the ground floor, property portfolios at intervals along this wall, rising in price as you advanced down the room. A front line set of desks in very much a military square, staffed by over zealous newbies, who would pounce on clients as soon as the phone stopped ringing. The desks would retreat in order of commerciality, until mine was reached, near the back opposite the staff loo. This was my overseas investment area. My oversized Mac took up much of the space, leaving just enough room for my vulnerable snow globe and a dusty money tree, a gift from my mother. Toby and Gordon had office space on a mezzanine floor further back above the client confidentiality suites. I could just about make out Toby's size 10's resting on his desk as he would watch his secretary Tamsin try out one of his new putters. He would show her how to clench the base of the club and focus on the ball before aiming at the empty mug resting on its side ten yards away. Tamsin was no golfer, but she complied and it kept him in good form. I had no illusions that the location of my desk was not in relation to my status within the firm. The young hitters, fresh from Uni, the cream with a consistency to match, occupy the front of house, their buying floor chatter is copious and not a little intimidating to some of the hesitant older clients that came through the door. If I am honest, it got to me - the hard sell and naked insincerity.

Don't get me wrong, I'm an agent, I do know how to sell, but I gave up that 'Dr Benton karate pose' on closing a deal long ago. It makes me cringe, the tactics used, the terminology, but it is just a reflection of the pressure, and that pressure has multiplied since I thought I could cut it as a hitter. I don't envy them at all, the commission league table is a battlefield, I have seen many burnouts and meteoric flights, and I have learnt to try and specialize, make my role tick over. So if you find it hard to steer a course to my desk, then the point is that I do most of my business over the phone, overseas and I don't need to be showcased.

The newbies and the hitters make enough fuss over themselves and clients, to just let me melt into the background, which is frankly where I like it. I have built up friendships in the past, but few are stayers, many are farmed out as relief to other branches, soon forgotten in the hinterland by dismissive regional managers. Others just don't hack it. The motto is unwritten, but it should be somewhere over the front door, probably in Latin, 'We Saw You Coming Sucker!'

It is always about the next sale, creating jargon for places that don't warrant such praise, inflating alternative usage and lifestyle choices to such a degree as to be pure fiction and as such unrecognisable from places we all know too well as to say the least, 'In need of some refurbishment'. We conjure dreams out of burdens, and make purses out of Sow's ears. We make money for people who already have it.

I know, I'm trying too hard to fall asleep, going to bed early was a dead give away, but it was worth a try. Gemma didn't bother to even read as her head hit the pillows, next thing she was in that foetal curl, doing that intermittent click that passes for a snore. It's different for me,

I want this too much, its a bit too confrontational. I mean what can I do to prevent this guy taking over my unconscious life? I turn and face her in the dark, then only to roll away later, wide awake and resentful of the precious time that passes. She is so lucky, no matter how crap her day was, and I do listen, she crashes like that, nothing comes between her and sleep time. It's preordained for her, she can sleep for Ireland, I fret for Ireland, if only I could distance myself from the petty hill of beans that amount to worry in my little life. I concentrate my gaze in the dark, constructing shapes in the inanimate gloom, I wish she would have let me stick those luminous stars to the ceiling, I could have been exploring the Big Dipper by now, but no, I had to put away childish things. Gemma fancies herself as an interior buff and those tacky stars didn't stand a chance. The crack in the doorway is lit by shadows from the trees outside, I can't sleep, it's official, so I extract myself from the covers without waking her. I grab my t-shirt and shorts from the Monk's chair on the landing and creep downstairs in the blue reflected shadows. The clock on the video says 2.00, great! The stove still has some embers left and I sit and watch them feeling more than a little sorry for myself. These dying lights manage to reach the picture rail, flickering off the shutters, down the back of the sofa. I'm no French knight intent on daylight, I want to be able to drift off and catch up with this Mr Unlive character. He must have other ideas, other people to bother, it's just not up to me when he appears. I can't conjure him or dream him up at will. Maybe that's not such a bad thing, after all he is more than a little odd and you don't even know what his intentions are. Wait a minute....I really need my bed now, this guy is not real and I am adding him to my already burgeoning worry list.

'Come back to bed.' Gemma.

'Coming.'

I slide in beside her, she turns out the light and it works, her settling words rub off on me and I'm gone in seconds, no visitations.

'I'm not cooking tonight.'

'Ok, I'll take you out for dinner.' She kisses me at the door, turns on her heel and is away, consumed by the rush hour. I won't be far behind her, going in a different direction, I do the compulsive ritual and grab my jacket, she has left a note on the windscreen in lipstick, 'miss me lover'. I do already, I always do, I can't ever tell her, for fear of letting my guard down. She holds the cards to my heart, if you saw her you would agree, I get in behind the wheel, not a little aroused by her lipstick, and just sit there at eight in the morning, thinking about her body and where I have been. This puts me in a good mood for work, even the journey is trouble free and I breeze past people I half know and like even less with the skill of a sniper.

Four hours in and I can get a response from a client in the U.S who is buying up land over here at a rate of knots, deconsecrated land that the church is selling off in rural parts of the north. She is a bit of a robot and never rises to the fact that I change my accent every time we talk on the phone. I suppose personality can't compete with currency, and, pardon the pun, she is acting with such grave intent that she neglects to notice any humour from me. I have been dealing with Jodi for so long that I have conjured her appearance in my mind down to the numeric buttons that seal her dress. This is wicked, but I do a lot of running around for her, with very little feedback, I always thought Americans were interested in the 'Old Country', but nope, not a drop of that has ever fallen down my well. Her e-mails are even be bleaker, succinct and to the point, I'll grant her, but verging on the frosty. I like to imagine what she looks like, glasses of course, hair tied back, you getting my stereotype here? Repressed naturally, but brimming with that film noir allure that you would dodge a bullet for. This slant is totally unprofessional, and I take it on the chin, she is a very important client, but it's the few crumbs she feeds me that make me wonder.

Another day punched in spending other people's money to buy land that they can sit on and squeeze the price of property in an already congested province with an inflated opinion of itself. Where did that come from? Well it's true, now more than ever, and I'm on the inside, so I know a little about what I'm on about.

I get home first and run a bath and half way through with my head under water and my back to the taps, she gets in. She strokes my sides on the surface and then holds my thighs.

We embrace like it was winter rain and we are parting on a platform for the last time. She presses against the tiles as I close in on her, my dark angel. We get dressed in silence, selfish in our completeness. I watch her pour into tight clothing as I tie my shoes. I should have booked ahead but it's a weekday and anyhow, I know the owner. The taxi is due in 15 minutes, or so they said.

We reach La Stanza at 8.15, the driver got lost somehow, and we paid for his mistake. Anyway, I hide my annoyance sufficiently and whisk Gemma up the steps to the restaurant. This is Hugo's flagship eatery, his first in a chain that comprises coffee shop concessions within bookshops and airports, to sandwich deliveries to busy offices. But this is where it all began, right here in Ballyhackamore. He got a loan from his Strandtown bank, sweet talked the manager and opened a sandwich bar. I don't know how many of these well-intentioned small businesses I've seen go belly up over the last 15 years, even the successful ones can over reach and 'rationalise' their business, but Hugo has been lucky. This place works on the premise of a mixture of European styles, served fresh and without fuss or bravado. The setting is ambient, and turned a four-year profit, leading to a refit in its fifth season. He has a Head Chef who worked alongside him in different restaurants over the last 20 years. That is rare and it shows, it's fair to say that he put this part of the Upper Newtownards Road on the culinary map.

We are shown to a booth in the window, I face Gemma and hold her hand across the table. She has been here before when we first started seeing each other, but not for ages. The menu has some 'old friends' that I will revisit, and he keeps a good cellar. Hugo is perched at the Waiter Service counter, craning over a calculator, with a half empty glass. He has put on weight since I last saw him, it makes me smile wryly. I suppose that's an occupational hazard, it gives my naivety a head start. The restaurant is filling up, the coat stand by the door is already brimming and different waiters are taking orders and making a fuss over people. I draw a heart in the jug of chilled water, as I pretend to mull over the familiar menu. Gemma fiddles with her dress and smiles at me, at all times some part of our bodies touch, even if it's just our toes. He's recognised me.

'Bones!' He shouts across and rises from his slouch. 'Did you get my email?'

'Yes Hugo.' He joins us... he has put on weight, success I suppose.

'Hello Emma!' Gemma's fake smile kicks in.

'It's Gemma.'

'I know...only kidding!' He kisses her cheek and settles beside her.

'Didn't think you would make it?'

'Don't see why not,'

'I bloody well hope so, it's been too long'

'How are you Hugo?'

'Fine, fine...how do I look?'

'Successful,'

'Successonaplate.com'

I try not to cringe, but it's so hard, especially with Gemma pressing her shoe leather into my heel. Hugo was my year, we probably do have so much to cover but she just wants to eat, I tried to kill two birds with one stone and over reached. I forgot to tell her about the reunion thing, what with the dreams and stuff it just got put at the back of my mind. Anyway it's ages away and I was going to give her plenty of notice.

'Let me order the wine for you. You will both love this.'

Hugo flags down one of his staff and sends them off to hunt out a bottle of one of his favourites.

'You remember Chuffy?'

The rusty clank of nickname recollection kick starts in my head.

'I do, real name Ryan Carew, 1st XI cricket, Money Box Committee, War Games Society and Chess Club.'

'Not bad old chum, you always did have good recall.'

'I remember he liked joining things, his picture cropped up more than most in our school magazine.'

'Well he will be in the obituary column in the next edition.'

'Chuffy dead...Chuffy Carew?'

How mortal is that? As if it couldn't happen to anyone protected by the golden glow of that summer of 1985.

'What happened?' I ask.

'You know he was a surveyor with Bannen Contracts?' asked Hugo

'Yes,'

'Bannen secured the regeneration work with Mylagan & Love.'

'That was an immense seven year project. I am representing them with an American client.'

'Chuffy headed up their Field Division, he could have sat back and let others get their boots dirty, but that wasn't his style. Anyway as I heard it, while pile driving, they came across a system of tunnels, which they believed might have been underground access points to the Chichester family estate which dated back to the late 1500's. These tunnels still had original timbers shoring them up and some had been carbon dated to an even earlier period. How's the wine?'

I look over at Gemma, she's not exactly glazing over, but it's in the post. I shrug as Hugo pours. This wine has legs. Poor old Chuffy.

'You two still with me?'

We nod, lean in his direction, hugging our glasses.

'Chuffy was in his element, and it got the better of him. He would stay later than most and use up all the arc light extensions to delve further into the tunnels. Poor bugger used to wade through all manner of shit down there, before the diggers and concrete filled in the gaps. He wanted to make a difference I suppose, find something relevant before the mall foundations bottomed out. Well it took hold of him, he took no notice of what time it was, the later the better in his eyes, fewer distractions at night, less people asking questions.'

Our main course arrives; we skipped the starter as we're both really hungry after the long delay for a taxi.

'As I was saying, Chuffy became obsessed with these tunnels and after a time he became convinced that he knew where they connected to. He began to map them, circumventing the regeneration plans with his own drawings of where the tunnels led. I think he was on to something, but from what I have been told it was wearing him out, as every time the Night Watchman caught up with him in the morning, he was drawn and haggard.'

'Poor old Chuffy.'

'I know. It began to interfere with the rest of his work, until he would only survey the site at night. His wife was distraught, believing at first that he was having an affair, then realising how he was withering away on a daily basis.'

I had opted for a safe choice - medium rare, salad and chips, the wine complemented everything. I must admit, Hugo had me hooked. Even Gemma was craning in.

'Turns out he must have caught some kind of infection down there, as it contaminated his blood supply, making him weaker and weaker.'

'Chuffy must have been about six foot two.'

'I know, but it floored him apparently, he even had a transfusion, but that seemed to drain away from him in days, until he was unable to visit the site anymore. I think that frustration finished him off more than anything. The diagnosis was consumption, he quickly deteriorated and without his supervision, the tunnels were filled in with concrete and are now lost. I heard he died in a fit of delirium, chanting schoolboy Latin.'

'I'm sorry, say that again?'

'He died of consumption. Some kind of Victorian disease.'

'I know that... but what was that about Latin?'

'Oh that, he was ranting Bones...towards the end poor guy!'

'His poor wife,' Gemma offers.

'I know Emma, it's a bugger of a blow. How was your steak?'

'Fine.'

Typical Hugo, always marching on to another topic, never willing to let any downcast atmosphere ruin a good meal.

'So I missed the funeral?'

'Me too, I only heard about it through Mr Beaumont.'

'You still call our old teachers Mr and sir?'

'I'm afraid so, especially when they dine here, these old buffers just don't fade away, they remember everything and take delight in recounting all manner of stories, especially about our year.'

'I suppose they can wax a bit on your wine.'

'I quite like it really, so much has passed, but they are constant reminders of what we got up to, beacons of our youth.'

'That's almost prosaic, Hugo!'

Beaumont was a bit scary from what I can remember, he would emphasise a point by wielding a hockey stick on his desk, I always seemed to retain information better in his class as a result.

'I won't keep you two, I can see Emma's in rapture with all this memory lane twaddle...not! I will see to your bill by way of recompense.'

'That's so sweet of you Hugo, you really shouldn't.'

'She's a honey Bones, look after that one.'

'Thanks Hugo, I will try.'

We take advantage of his hospitality, enjoying late night drinks at the window table as the restaurant revolved around us. Later we pour ourselves into a passing taxi and head for other side of town.

2

I slept a little too well last night, can't remember a thing, certainly not disturbed or visited, got up once to go to the loo without waking her, but nothing else to report. Hugo was generous, I can't help but think about Chuffy wasting away like that. I know that we didn't keep in touch, but I saw him about 18 months ago, jogging past Osbourne Park. I was grid locked as usual and he looked in good shape. Anyway I'm out of porridge and running late, no time to check out the mail, looks like a bunch of circulars anyway.

The wipers scrape in time to Nostalgia FM, "IF I HAD A PHOTOGRAPH OF YOU, OR SOMETHING TO REMIND ME...I WOULDN'T SPEND MY LIFE JUST WAITING". I know it's early, but did I really like 'Flock Of Seagulls' that much? Okay, I bought the 12" of 'I Ran', but that was really meant for Trudy Lyles, who used to meet me in the crawl space under the Ulster Museum for a smoke and a snog. Anyway she never got the record as I caused a little unpleasantness at her parents, by being sick all over their downstairs loo. What happened to Trudy? I still have the single though in a trunk ready to play on the day I finally lose it.

My boss is giving us a meeting. Gordon is about three years older than me. We have worked together in some capacity for about fifteen years and I have come to know his style of delivery; it's slow and deliberate, but gets there. It can be frustrating to the young blades who are anxious to leave the traps, but I've learnt to adapt to his way of doing things. I get back to my desk and email Hugo, thanking him again before I forget. I ask him to put my name down for the reunion and to keep in touch.

I will ring Jodi, our American land grabber later, even though she probably never sleeps and walks the eastern seaboard at night devouring souls in nothing but a shift. The rest of the morning is a round robin of familiar voices down the phone, signing off emails and following up clients. When lunchtime comes, I head for Café Anjou.

All the good seats outside are always taken by the young and the pram ridden. I don't mind queuing, the coffee is worth it, they know me here and are always cheerful and friendly. Tanya gives me my large mug of regular. For some reason I ask her for a phone book, she hunts around and brings a battered copy to my table with a Panini Wrap. It struck me to look up Unlive in the book. Don't ask, it just seemed the thing to do. I'm not even in the book so why should I expect such a strange name to be there? Leafing through I find myself looking up names I know, only to land on Carew. There it is, Ryan Carew, 41 Valmont Road, 02890666901. What are you going to do about this? You hadn't spoken to him in years and you certainly don't know his wife Dinah. Anyway I take a note of his number and head for 'U'. Tanya gives me a free refill and I chomp away at the wrap. There are not many 'U's as you can probably guess and Unlive is not among them. Well that would have been a comedy moment, expecting to find a name of a guy who only appears in my dreams in the phone book. I leave the book on the counter and ask Tanya for a Yellow Pages, she gives me that 'What did your last one die of' look, that begs me to see how busy she is.

'When you get a chance.'

I sit down to ease the congestion. I know she works really hard, it's part of the atmosphere that makes this place tick. I love just leaning over a mug watching everyone, taking time out to breathe it all in, to just linger and drift in my head. The Yellow Pages thud in front of me, Tanya gives me that cheeky grin and turns on her heel back to the serving counter. A glance at my watch tells me to drain this mug and have a quick look in the book. I look up tour guides, City tour guides, plenty of those, alphabetical of course. My finger lands on a single line, near the end, an afterthought really. Resurgam Tours ABTA reg. 13 Joys Entry, Belfast BT1 9AW. Tel. 02890247355. Night tours.

I have pretty much cleared my desk by mid afternoon, so I wander off to the records department to check out a hunch. I bump into Sandra Morton and sit on her desk for a while chewing the fat. Sandra is another long stay patient, about my age, maybe a wee bit older, I text her on her birthday and she makes me discs of eighties music she thinks that I'm still into. Sandra has been holding a torch for so long now that I have forgotten the guy's name. She is good looking and in great shape, but I think deep down she is afraid to be happy, with nothing to moan about. Does this sound harsh? I have so much time for her. Where others bitch, I listen, but its hopeless she just can't play up her good points. Sandra usually sends me back to my desk worried about my lack of Pension cover or other mortal insecurities. But not today, I hand her back the key to the Records Office and head back to my desk with some old facsimiles relating to central Belfast. These books are split into Wards, with old names for areas of Belfast like Cromac or Farsett. Many of these formative Land Registry books have been destroyed by fire or lost; those that remain have long since been transferred on to disk. The records coincide with Census dates, every ten years or so. I scroll my way through the 1850 edition, each ward is mapped and hand written, the limits and boundaries of ownership are clearly marked out on the pages. The script and detail are so painstaking, even at this early date; the pages feature sponsors and advertisers who have premises related to appropriate pages. I come to the section I want, the border of the page is lined with ads for Vintners and Sparkling Mineral Merchants as well as Linen manufacturers. Joys Entry is clearly visible, its name unchanged. Even back then, the area was a congested sprawl of business premises, workshops and public houses. The crooked line of the entry is cross-sectioned by the squares of different premises, the owner and present incumbent is listed clearly in the border of each page. I reach number

13, it would be that number of course, Mr Titus Unlive, Occupation, Linen Merchant, Issue 0. Well he did point out his relative in the King Billy wig, but that painting was from an even earlier period, when Joys Entry would have been part of the landscaped gardens on the Chichester estate. The first name must be one that the family have cherished and handed down to different generations. That's what it is, these wealthy families liked to keep quirky things like that. Many if not all these Linen manufacturers where exiled French Huguenot stock and therefore victims of persecution and as a result tended to be cliquish and secretive. It seems he must have lived over the premises. After all he had at that date no family, so no reason to move to the more prosperous suburbs such as Mount Pottinger across the river. I close the 1850 edition and reach for the 1800 disk. The text and script in this edition are much different from the last, far less commercial, every detail is hand written, more like a ledger. Again the wards are clearly laid out and the outline from the old Linen Hall, where the City Hall is now is easy to follow, fewer streets with familiar names to us today. Joys Entry is there of course, the dog leg shape, half way up is number 13. The property is smaller looking with fewer outbuildings, its border is in bold ink, with entrances front and back. The margin contains the names of owner/tenants, number 13 belongs to a Mr Titus Unlive, Occupation, Linen Merchant, Issue 0.

Orton taps me on the shoulder, 'You all right love? Someone just walk over your grave?'

'What?...Yeah...I'm fine.'

'Didn't hear me ringing you then?'

'No, sorry mate, was miles away.'

'Jodi was on the blower for you. Must have been important for her to call?'

'Yeah...thanks, I'll email her now.'

I didn't hear the phone at all. I was just staring at this page, the name written so finely with some kind of quill. Unlive at that address in 1800, his family, wait a minute, what family? Issue 0 remember? No children. They must have married late, settled their business affairs and married a younger woman. Of course, back then, mortality rates were so high that a younger wife could come to term with more pregnancies and cope with stillbirths and infant deaths. It must be the case that Unlive men married late and played catch up! They held on to their property for so long by stealth and late breeding, the Births Register is bound to testify to this. But what if the real reason is that Mr Unlive is somehow not dying and living on to enjoy his property for much longer than any ordinary person should hope to do so. That's bollocks! Snap out of it, the answer is plain; shrewd avoidance of some kind of inheritance tax is at play here, business savvy nothing sinister. This family home has been handed down to different generations of the Unlive family since they first arrived from France in the 1780's. Refugees who got a foothold in the heart of Belfast and worked hard to embellish and keep hold of their property.

Behind me there's an array of wall clocks displaying the time in different cities of the world. This is a piece of provincial delusion that makes me chuckle. Anyhow I can see that it must be 12.25 in New York, I'll ring Jodi. What voice will I put on for her? Stuff that, this whole Unlive thing has given me the jitters. Where's my diary? She seems different today, can I even say upbeat? It's as if she knows something about me that she didn't before and has thawed in attitude towards me. I find all this a bit hard to take, I want my Nurse Diesel Jodi back, the severe matron of the night who walks the eastern seaboard blah...blah...blah. It takes her ages to get to the point, not like her at all, if I didn't know better I'd say she was flirting with me. She is my first point of contact with the U.S investors in the Mylagan & Love development. Turnkey city apartments under a glass canopy in the heart of Belfast. A prime location for city living, with a good rate of return for any investor/ landlord. Well that's the spiel, in actual fact it's a claggy mess of bog being pile driven on a daily basis. This is where Ryan Carew poured his life away, fretting over tunnels that ran under the entries within Ann Street. Jodi's client wants to buy into it, they have Irish roots, and the climate is now right. She is positively purring now in American, very disconcerting. I look at the mouthpiece, wonder what the hell has changed. She never chewed any fat before, so why all the chatter about the view from her window and what's the weather like with me? I fall into her girlie chat and take all the details I can about her client. Later, when I regain composure I decide that I liked the severe version better. My illusions are just about intact.

I walk over to Orton's desk.

'Did you speak to Jodi much?' He asks.

'Sort of, she said she was heading out later to some Jazz club. That's more than I have got from her in three years.'

'She was in the mood to chat I guess,'

'Hmm...not like my girl at all.'

'Your girl?'

'The girl I thought I knew, I mean.'

'Whatever dear, I'm heading for a pint, fancy one?'

'I might catch you later, where you going?'

'Quell Dommage,'

'You big poof.'

'Well I don't see you getting any other offers!'

I glance at my phone, 5.40, no texts, I'll ring Gemma from the pub.

'Come on then, grab your coat, you've pulled.'

'Hark at you, international playboy!'

I like Orton, he's so straight for a gay guy, if you get my meaning. He flirts with everybody and his friends call him Blanche, but he likes me to call him by his surname, as he says it gives him strength. I take this as a compliment as no one else is allowed to call him Orton, for fear of his cutting remarks. He is a femme, and you can tell he plucks in all the right places, quite suits him really, he takes his time over his appearance and acts as a counter balance to the ruddy faced pin-stripers who were so eager to leave the womb with a rugger ball under one arm.

We cross the street and walk about half a mile to Quell Dommage. This is definitely Orton's local, judging by the coven that meet there and he is welcomed at the bar by his stage name.

'Blanche darling what will it be?'

'The usual Freddie.'

'And the gentleman?'

'A glass of house red please.'

I decide to dispense with the idle office banter and just watch the room, taking in the Friday crowd, shackles off, ready for the weekend. Orton pays and we thread through the tight bodies, trying not to spill. We reach a seated podium in the window where his friends are.

'Daahling...thought you were dead!'

'This is Ian, also known as Ina. This is David, also known as Sally.'

'Budge up love, me heels are killing me!' Blanche exclaims.

'Well, what have we here, is she trying to turn you love?'

Ina's eyes burn with a recalcitrant air.

'Don't be silly, we work together.'

'And what do they call you?' David/Sally purrs as I sit beside her, I tell her my name and she looks interested, looking me up and down as I recount how long I've known Orton. It turns out Sally is a Locksmith with the smoothest hands in what is a precision occupation. 'She' swears by Swafega, it regenerates the pores while the smell comfortingly reminds her of her late father.

'I'm always on call. I can sneak you in anywhere!'

This loosely veiled banter carries on as I sip my glass and look periodically at my phone for the relief of a text. Orton and Ina polish off their drinks and I offer to buy the next round.

'Thank you darling, you can stay a whole week!' Sally definitely likes me. I try not to look like a mincer as I make my way to the bar, certain that my every move is being lock picked by the Sisterhood. I wait in the crush at the counter, my elbows soaking up the residue from the pinioned beer mats. I fumble awkwardly and phone Gemma. She has left it on answer phone, barely audible, I leave a message.

'You know that Nesta and Joan have split up?' Ina declares as I return with a full tray. I try to stifle a smile as I hear more nicknames. Orton gives me a knowing glare and asks in concerned tones as to what became of their relationship.

'Turns out Nasty Nesta was dropping anchor in some other bay,'
'Really, anyone I know?'
'One of those fit cycling postmen with a boy in every post code.'
'The bitch, Joan in bits I suppose?'
'Joan moved out, can you believe it, out of the garden flat!'
'That was her pride and joy, the nights we have had in there.'
'I know...she is back with her mother in the New Lodge.'

Now I'm in trouble here, this is great stuff, I mean hilarious but I can't let on or they will eat me for sure. I whip out my phone for the hundredth time.

'You expecting a call love?' says Sally, stroking my thigh. A rouge complexion I've never worn comes over me as I alter my stance.

'Yeah...nothing in for tea, so I might have to slip away.'
'You are such a shite liar,' under my breath.
'He's a good boy, can you cook as well as you look?' Ina asks.
'I get by I suppose, I mean I can usually rustle something up.'

Just as Ina composes another double entendre, my phone lights up.

'Hiya love, how are you?' I blurt. 'Can just about hear you.' I press the phone as tight to my ear as a crucifix. This is my chance for closure, I shrug and try to look dejected before saying,

'Leave it with me, M&S are still open, I can pop in on the way home.' I hang up.

'I have to go I'm afraid. It was nice to meet you both. I'll see you Monday Orton, have a good weekend!'

'Be good darling,' says Sally and winks. 'And if you can't, be bad with me!'

She looks like she is used to getting the last word, so I leave it at that. I mean if that was what did it for me, then I was well in.

I press past them and on through the bar room throng, deafened by the ephemeral dross being relayed by multiple flat screens in the ceiling.

Outside, the overspill from the bar, the suits, stubbing out cigarettes on wheelie bins, sitting under awnings, posing in the drizzle with their flat lagers. God I'm glad to be out of there, too many fake smiles on people I half know, all that after hours mock sincerity.

It's getting near twilight as I speed up from Stranmillis lights, the climb in the road, I've done it a million times, the Gate Lodge at Bladon that I always wanted to live in is up for rent and Ryan Carew is jogging down the drive. Rewind!...he's dead!...very dead! I mount the pavement at Deramore, loud beeps and dirty looks from pissed off drivers in my ears. It must be at least 200 yards from where I saw him, I'm in a suit for god's sake, I'm not going to catch him no matter how fast I run in these shoes. So I'm standing there arms akimbo, with Friday revellers and late office returnees buzzing by, the looks they give, you'd think I had two heads.

I'm still shaking my solitary head as I turn the key. Gemma's got company, Trish and Paula from Accounts. They are well ensconced on the sofa, on their second bottle by the look of it; I will have some catching up to do. Gemma reaches up and pulls my tie.

'Long day lover?'

'Interesting...have you eaten yet?'

'We got bored waiting for you and ordered in,'

'Chinese I hope?'

'Should be enough to go around anyway.' I grab a glass from the cupboard and join them.

"DID I DREAM ...YOU DREAMED ABOUT ME
WHERE YOU HERE WHEN I WAS FORCED TO LOVE..."

No not Mr Unlive unfortunately, but a long lost classic from This Mortal Coil, you guessed it, Nostalgia FM.

Transports of delight soon fade away beyond the cereal bowl and out the window as the weather report and the ad for expanded leather sofa reductions kick in. It being a Saturday I can nurse this groggy head at my leisure. Plenty of filter coffee and toast to fortify this hangover, I caught up with the girls last night and overtook them at the lights. It must have been some kind of release valve, but I remember going out to buy more wine and having in depth discussions with the bouncer at the Bot Off Licence. I didn't give in though and treat myself to one of those caravan kebabs, the blaring generator of which bounces off the backyard walls down Wellington Park to our flat. I vaguely remember some pretty one-sided discussions about male sexuality with Trish and Paula, nothing outlandish, I fought our corner, so to speak. Trish got a taxi late on and Paula stayed. She is now laying claim to the bathroom when I need to go the most. I pour out some more coffee and bring a cup to Gemma.

'How's the head darlin?' Two arms stretch at length from the covers, a foot pops out the other end.

'Bit rough, your snoring didn't help things much, I had to bunk up with Paula at one stage, you were so bad.'

'I missed that completely, totally out cold. Here's a coffee, get that down you and I will make us all breakfast.'

'Morning Paula, I see you helped yourself to one of my shirts.'

'Knew you wouldn't mind. I thought it was the least you could provide considering how pissed you were.'

'Was I that bad?'

'Just a bit, I take it you don't remember making a pass at Trish?'

'Bugger...you're joking aren't you? Trish?'

'Why do you think she left so early?'

'If so why didn't you go with her?' I ask.

'It didn't bother me, and anyway you're not my type.' Jesus! I turn away from her, and pause at the window.

'You can't look at me now, not even in your shirt, don't I do it justice?'

'It's not that at all. Anyway I'm not your type, you know what I mean.'

'You are so easy to wind up. Trish had to go early, she has to pack for her holiday.'

'So I didn't make a pass at her?'

'You flirted, you always do, but we are used to it.'

'And Gemma?'

'She was too busy trying to fight me off every time she went to fill up the glasses in the kitchen.'

'Stop it Paula, I can't unravel fact from fiction now.'

'Good,' Paula leans over the breakfast table, my old shirt she's wearing riding up and kisses me squarely on the lips. 'Any chance of some breakfast?'

'I'll get started, there's some bacon I bought last night and plenty of eggs.'

I go for a pee and Paula starts cutting the rind off the bacon, a total waste in my view as it can be the tastiest bit when crispy.

'So Gemma bunked up with you then?'

'There you go, honestly, your imagination, did you think of that while you were having a wee?'

'Maybe.' The Lads Mag elemental is definitely out of the bottle, and I am playing out some flirty fantasy with my girlfriend's best mate over the frying pan.

'We kissed ages ago, at a taxi rank after one of the Christmas parties. I guess we were both drunk, but then not a little curious, as I have always found Gemma to be so gorgeous.'

This is distracting me from my culinary duties and the bacon splashes me as it begins to foam.

'It never got in the way of anything, we kissed that's all, we never spoke of it again until last night. What with you snoring so much, she couldn't sleep, so she slid in beside me. We talked about everything, we always do.'

'Then?' She stalled.

'We started kissing again.'

I am standing with pan and spatula listening to a rendition of girl on girl action between Gemma and Paula. Ok it was kissing, but what do I say, how do I react?

'How do you like your eggs?' is all that comes out of my mouth.

'Easy over.'

What the hell does that mean? Come on. Its some kind of Amerispeak that I should email Jodi to explain. On second thoughts that's probably not such a good idea, given the mood swings with that lady at the present time.

'Morning!'

We both look at Gemma, Paula with that 'cream licked look' and me with the 'who left the cake out in the rain' look.

'Bacon smells good!' she says politely. Its probably stuck to the non-stick for all the attention I have been giving it, but no, it's still very salvageable. I rinse out the filter pot and boil up some water. Paula heads off to get dressed and smiles past Gemma as she does so.

'How you feeling love?' Gemma asks.

'Bit vulnerable I suppose.'

'You hit the wine pretty hard last night, did something rattle your cage?

'You wouldn't believe it what with all the things going on around here!'

'Such as?'

'Maybe you and Paula kissing while I was snoring next door?'

'Oh that.'

'Yes that, when were you going to tell me?'

'I wasn't, far as I can see it's nothing to do with you.'

'Well ok then...fine.'

'I can see you are hurt, but that's just your pride, you did flirt with the two of them a lot last night, I just went that bit further.'

'So you were curious then?'

'You fancy me, so does Paula, I just wanted to see what it felt like with her.'

'Ever since the Christmas party? You snogged her then?'

'We were drunk, it just felt right, I'm not going to run away with her, we're not Lipstick Lezza's, just curious, I'll put in the toast shall I?'

Later, I manage to bow out of watching Gemma's retail therapy, I take my car and drive with a half intent to Oldtownbreda cemetery. I know which turn to take as I frequented this place at intervals on teenage drinking bouts. All that shivering with a flat tin of Harp, sucking on fags, trying to impress wee girls in the damp. The side gate located in the wall at the top of the hill, two sombre Cypress trees nod towards the graves of the great and the good. This approach seems steeper now it's almost laughable to think of the lack of respect that the developers showed, building crappy homes almost right up to the gates. That's a bit rich coming from me, the seasoned estate agent, who would have sold his maiden aunt for a lucrative commission. I close the gate behind me and pace out the perimeter of the graveyard. I never took it in before, too busy trying to balance a tin on a headstone while fiddling with an awkward blouse or jacket button. The old internments with grand facades hard by the enclosure walls, family vaults with broken columns signifying loved ones cut down in their prime. I marvel in the solemn richness of the detail spent here. These people did their utmost to be remembered, they never made provision for erosion or the vandals, too busy trying to out-column one another in differing styles that the elements have slimed and blackened. Crunching along the gravel, the sleek lick of weedy grass carpets around crooked headstones, leading me to the church and the new cemetery beyond. What a contrast, the sheen of black marble, gold inscriptions, these 'beds for the dead', the glare of white shingle, stained from rusting vases with petrified bouquets. The trees like everything else are manicured here, the edged pathways are neat and each plot is uniform, at the end of each row is a bench with a bin. It will take me a while, but I have time, I can search for Ryan Carew, his will be a fresh plot, maybe he doesn't have a headstone yet? I can always ask one of the gardeners. Semple, Turkington, Carruthers, Smylie, these are all recent, judging by the condition of the marble edifice on each. As I reach the far end, I find two fresh plots, one still hollowed out with Astroturf covering the displaced soil. The other has a simple wood stained cross, Carew, Ryan, 28th Nov 1966 - 2nd Dec 2006. As simple as that, no sentiment, no hearts and flowers, just a peg in the damp earth, 'Poor Old Chuffy' indeed. I suppose I needed closure, its not as if we kept in touch, this starkness rounds it off for me. I have been too caught up in myself, letting my imagination off the hook. If I still smoked, I would have one now, the perfect time to waste a few minutes in quiet reflection, but I don't, so I make do with perching on a damp bench beside the wheelie bin full of dead stems and offerings. A winter sun tires above the yew trees and calls it a day at the gateway, signalling time for me to stretch and head back to reality.

Monday comes, and it's a team meeting with Gordon first thing. The usual stuff, nothing that I haven't heard before, expletives are exhausted as they are bandied about the Board Room, bouncing off the Yellow Pack newbies in the hope that they will come up with some untried method of reaching ever heightening sales targets. How green I once was, as green as Gordon's ill fitting cardigan, his motivational talk not backed up with the natty attire expected by the Hitters in the room. They half listen as a result, and I don't expect him to have witnessed the grimaces they make, I made them too, when I was in love with myself. Gordon is the Buffer zone, I came to realise this, he is my connection with the reasons why I came into this work. I would have forgotten it long ago, but for him, his phlegmatic delivery falls short of ambition, which is seen as a weakness, but I like it, so I always listen.

Back at my desk, an email from The Reform Club - my deposit required for Class Reunion Dinner. God is it that time already? The dinner is only seven days away. I'll send them a cheque. The menu unravels as I browse down the page; confit of this, seared heart of that, an unrivalled amount of food snobbery that Hugo would balk at. The itinerary peels like the inter-period school bell, climaxing with the night tour, led by Mr Unlive of Resurgam Tours. That name again, not exactly as common as Smith or McClure, it seems to flow through every part of what I am now, both awake or sleeping. Can't see the need for a tour myself, I mean a bunch of half arsed acquaintances dressed up like penguins, full of veal and Port wine, traipsing down dark entries in the middle of town? Well maybe the air might do some good, we can always beak off and head for one of the many secluded pubs. A night tour in the drizzle though? Not the most appealing so close to Christmas, with everyone bumping off each other trying to keep their purchases dry. I sign off a cheque and leave it in my out tray.

3

'You are making connections methinks, and you have so much that you want to ask me,'

'Yes,' I struggle.

'All in good time. Time is something I know so much about. I have been blessed with it.'

'Why am I here?'

'Our paths would have crossed soon anyway. I have just conjoined us now so that we could have this conversation. I am in your way, in a manner of speaking. At least the authority that I live under is in your way.'

'You're in my way?'

'Yes, the people you represent wished to demolish my home and replace it with a glass domed retail citadel. With underground parking no less!'

'You mean Mylagan & Love?'

'Entirely, can I tempt you to have some more sack?'

'Yes please.'

He pours with a steady hand and offers me the refill. I've heard of out of office hours visits, but this is new territory, an out of hours dream visitation by a hostile client with an agenda that I can't reconcile.

'Please don't concern yourself, you mean well and anyway Verily has kicked your demolition proposal into touch, as you might say.'
Verily! Of course, she's even more formidable than this character.

'I undertook the role before I was aware that your building was listed. All the other buildings in Joys Entry are uninhabited, warehouses and the like.'

'You weren't to know when you started your enquiries, your client wanted the land, and you were only acting on their behalf. I quite understand, I would do the same.'

The velvet pull of the fine sack reacts with my neck muscles, relaxing me. He notes my ease and throws a log on the grate before sitting opposite me.

'I want to tell you more, but as you have found our conversations can be interrupted by your waking hours, this makes my story more staccato, but you will get the message in the end.'

'Can you tell me more about yourself?' I ask, growing in confidence.

'You have already learnt that my family have owned this property for some considerable period of time.'

'Ehh...yes, something like two hundred years, am I right?'

'That is correct, I think you have come to your own assumption with regard to the fact that under closer inspection, my issue has always remained 0 and yet my family has retained this building for that length of time.'

'I put it down to creative accounting.'

This quip is not wasted on him. He leans forward in his chair and his countenance has changed dramatically.

'Have you ever heard of the Kingsevil?'

'I guess there have been some nasty monarchs, like John or Henry VIII, they stand out as kinda evil.'

'Let me explain it better for you so that you might learn. Every anointed king, under the eyes of god has the power to touch or rub away any ailment or illness through holy oils and the placement on the body of specially minted coins. I was the Keeper of the Kingsevil at the court of Charles II.'

'Mother of God!' with an emphasis on the G! I thought the bi-millennial occupation was hard enough to take in, but this!

'How well do you know your history?' He enquires.

'I did it for A-level at Cropredy.'

I only got an E because I skipped one of the papers to skive off with

Rawnsley of course.

'No matter, I served at court prior to the plague and the great fire in the reign of his late Majesty.'

I find myself nodding in agreement - it must be the wine.

'Yes I have heard about the fire, some baker's oven that overheated and burnt half of London.' The ensuing property boom would have been the making of me, if only I was around to see it.

'The plague and the fire were seen as divine retribution for the salacious court overseen by his late Majesty. The plague was no respecter of rank; the rich fled, the poor were left to throw the weak and the sick out into the street to die if they suspected pestilence had taken its grip on them. It took with it my own father and mother. Both Huguenot refugees from La Rochelle, where Louis XIV had revoked the edict of Nantes, guaranteeing the religious freedom of all Protestants on mainland Europe.'

Prods eh! That'll be it. You just have to scrape the surface and the old religious card is played!

'I'm sure I do not know what you mean, even though you are just thinking it!'

He can read my thoughts as well...Brilliant!

'After the fire, the King looked kindly upon me and instructed me to undertake the role my father had so diligently provided, as Keeper of the Kingsevil oil. This role I did perform until his late Majesty's conversion on his deathbed to the Church of Rome in 1685. I could not in all conscience serve in that role under the late King's brother, James, who was openly Catholic and who had constructed a chapel within the palace of Whitehall. It was with great delight that a protestant wind brought me hither to Ireland with William of Orange in 1690. I was with his entourage, but more importantly I still had the secret Kingsevil oil. The new regime looked upon Kingsevil as Popish trickery. I kept the oil, I must admit I kept some of the coins as keepsakes. I was retained as

Apothecary within King William's retinue while he was on campaign in Ireland. I witnessed Schomberg's death, the poor fellow cut through like a pin-cushion, beyond any help I could offer. The King's remorse at his loss was tempered by a fit of asthma.'

'You must bide with me here,' I say, 'this fine wine is helping me, but do you honestly expect me to believe that you have been taking some kind of medicine that prolongs life?'

'I do and I am, I would not lie on this matter or any other.'

Why should he make this up? What has he to gain by rhyming off this kind of tale?

'It's an incredible story,' I hear myself say. 'You decided to make contact with me first, do I have a role in this other than the estate agent who wanted to demolish your home?'

'I said before that you were acting with honest intentions, and that I held no grudge against you for doing that.'

'Then why did you go to such lengths to contact me?'

'I was fortunate to have Verily and the Built Heritage people on my side, you recall it was her who did all the fighting for me, she had the fortitude and happily my property was listed. The underlying reason is the client you represent.'

'You mean Mylagan & Love?'

'No, the Americans.'

'So you know that we have American investors in the development? You honestly think that they are bad for business?'

'What do you know of these investors?'

He asks as if he already knew without me answering. In reality Jodi was the keeper of their implacable Iron Curtain. All along I had been fed crumbs across the pond by rich ex-pats buying up deconsecrated and brown field sites all over Ireland. Something tells me that this is bigger than I can handle, he has probably sensed this emotion and his posture backs down as he strokes what he calls his 'Firedogs' and stares into the dwindling firelight.

SENTIMENTAL POWERS WON'T HELP YOU NOW SO SKIP THE HEARTS AND FLOWERS AND THE IVORY TOWERS

The best lines Martin Fry ever wrote grow louder from my Bose clock radio. Trevor Horne produced the Lexicon Of Love and it's a damn fine album.

Jodi Penn, 36, is a Client Consultant with Richelieu-Mazarin Holdings. Her office is on the 4th floor at 8 E 43rd St. New York. The building is a nod to the Venetian style, with Verona balconies that would leave little scope for Juliet to climb down to her Romeo. She happens to work in the smallest office block in the mid-town area, the building being protected as a place of significant architectural merit. She has been with the company for seven years, she commutes from Hackensack and Grand Central Station is just five blocks away. She is blonde, 5ft 4, but appears much taller in the retro heels she likes to wear. She is slim and single and likes wearing figure-hugging dresses. Back home in Hackensack she still lives with her parents, Wally and Freda Penn. Wally is a Teamster delegate with forty years under his belt. Freda supplies home baked goods to micro-grocers in the local district. Jodi may be single, but that's because it suits her. She has to fend off offers on a regular basis from both sexes. Her reasons are integral to her and she just doesn't see the rush to settle down. Jodi is taking some heat this morning from her immediate superior, Francine Wanamaker. Francine is 50, answers to Paul Rideout at Overseas Development, and he is anxious as why they have not heard from their Irish contact Ryan Carew for the past three weeks. Smarting from this, Jodi fires off a salvo to Mylagan & Love. She is so annoyed that she forgets the five-hour time difference. An out of office hours email rebounds onto her screen. It's a Friday and Mylagan

& Love being developers close at 4.30 pm Irish time. She takes the back stairs and congregates with the smokers at the side street building exit.

'Morning Jodi, you sure look pissed at something,' says Ray from Accounts.

'I know, I'm the worst at hiding shit, can I have a light?'

'Be my guest.'

'I mean the guy might have been on vacation or something, but no, she has to take it out on me, just because Rideout balled her out.'

'That's it honey, get it out, out of your system, out in the street, let it go.'

'Assholes!'

'Damn lady, such a dirty word from a sweet mouth.'

'Well they are, the lot of them, lashing out at other people to justify themselves.'

'The way of the World Jodi, find someone else to blame. This city wasn't built on sentiment.'

'It was built on sediment Lady!'

'Thanks for that Ray.'

'You're welcome Sweet Cheeks.'

Jodi stubs the butt beneath her square-toed mule and heads for the Bagel World across the street.

'Hey pretty lady, you want your usual?'

'Thanks Emile, with a large cup of Joe today,'

'Coming right up.'

She pays and runs back across the street and through the cool marble foyer with a bust of Machiavelli at one end, a homage to the Doge's Palace in St. Marks Square. She unwraps the bagel at her desk, the coffee alters her mood before she even takes a sip. The bagel is history.

If Carew is on vacation, then who is carrying the torch over there? Carew was on the ground, got his hands dirty, the only other contact I have is that sarcastic creep at Lydon & Dye. What was his bloody name?

She scrolls down her inbox history stalling at Will Donaghoe. He's the sleeked little termite that thinks I can't tell his accent changes every time I speak on the phone. Which is as little as possible if I can help it. I'm in the mood to take on that creep today, but calm it Jodi, you heard Ray. Donaghoe, the little Irish bogman, he'll do. I'll play his little game, I'll be the cupcake people know I can be, freak him out completely, flirt even. I suppose I could just ring their office, that Gordon guy is bound to be there after hours. Maybe I should just email the creep and see what comes.

Later Francine does a drive-by along Jodi's desk with the olive branch expression she has perfected since the guilt kicked in about her innocence in this affair. Francine can't stay annoyed for long which is to Jodi's credit.

'Jodi I'm catching some fire over this Irish deal. You must understand that the Partners want to sew up this matter in Belfast as soon as possible.'

'I totally understand. I have been in on this since the beginning. Carew is usually so prompt at getting back to us. I just thought he might have been away or unwell.'

'If Carew can't help us, have you someone else to fall back on?'

'Yeah…I have been in contact with an agent over there, he's a Schmuck, but he's reliable.'

'Good, then we can clear this up soon.'

Francine looks relieved as she turns away from Jodi's desk and returns to the 10th floor. Just then, Karla appears looking for the mid-western account file.

'Hey girl, what say you and me head for a drink after work.'

'You know what Karla, I would love that.'

'I know this jazz club in Greenwich Village, if you have the time.'

'Yes, lets do that, we can make ourselves up here then head out.'

'See you later.'

Let me see, this is Friday, what time is it in Ireland? 5.35, I might catch Donaghoe if I'm quick. Jodi dials the international code and the number for Lydon & Dye. She gets through to some guy called Orton who says Donaghoe is not at his desk, but hasn't gone home just yet. She tells Orton to get him to ring her. Moments later a speculative email arrives from Donaghoe. It smacks of last thing on a Friday sentiment.

Hi Jodi,
Are you looking forward to the jazz this weekend?
(THIS SAD SACK IS JUST QUOTING WHAT I TOLD ORTON)
Anyway let me know what I can help you with and I will get onto it on Monday.
Cheers, Will.

Hi Will,
It's probably nothing, but we haven't heard from our Mylagan contact, Ryan Carew for a few weeks. Are we any closer to securing the last property on that development?
Regards, Jodi.

Dinah Carew like most others is unsure what interval of time has to elapse before taking the cards down. The polite and the well-meaning have long since vouchsafed help and company. The notes of sympathy have migrated from the mantelpiece in the living room, behind the family photos on the writing desk, to the windowsill in the dining room. She has enough frozen casseroles and lasagnes cooked by her mother and stored safely, to feed all-comers for the duration. The last three weeks have showcased her resolve and forbearance. Dinah is a pragmatist, she gets it from her father's side, her dad was the eldest of seven. Her father's father was an alcoholic, rendering his contribution to the family as negligible. The eldest boys took on the roles of provider, taking ill paid manual roles to help out their mother. Dinah's grandmother lived long enough to see her boys grow, she instilled affection equally, and a sense of what was just and true. Dinah Carew is a widow at 38 with two girls, Kirstie aged 11 and Paige aged 9. She knows the mortgage on the house is now paid in full and that Ryan had a considerable life insurance policy. She knows that the financial window dressing is background noise to the fact that Ryan is dead. Her practical nature tells her that she will have to clear out his wardrobe, the charity shop will get its share, but not yet. She won't be parted from the denim jacket he wore to ask her out. Her girls ask her questions every night, some of which she struggles to answer, but she steals herself and finds a way. Ryan left grass that needs mowed on three sides of their house. His 7-series BMW takes up most of the driveway. The conservatory roof still has his finger marks in the putty where he replaced the corrugated panes. His smiling face in a montage of things that mattered as a family, the alphabet that spelt out love on a fridge magnet, his favourite cereal, half full, a spare seat at the breakfast table. His shaving balm, shoes under the bed, the mail order stuff with his name on it, his vinyl in the attic, the school team photographs framing the hallway. Dinah knows this is just the start, in her job as a counsellor she is all too familiar with the progression of grief. She has the kids to think about, to be strong for, she can channel strength through them. They will go on, everything does and they are certainly not alone. But when they are finally asleep and all help has gone home for the day, she can question things in the dark. Why have you gone? What really happened to you?

The answers won't come easy, and certainly not now from Ryan. But they are out there in the ether. One man knows why Ryan Carew paid the ultimate price.

4

'I really hate these things.'

'Here let me give it a try.' Gemma takes my bow tie and cradles my neck.

'You're as bad as me!'

'Didn't they give you a ready made one at the hire shop?'

'Yes, they offered me one.'

'Well you should have taken it.'

'I know, but I thought it would look tacky.'

'At least you would have your life back to get on with other things!'

'You win, pass me the box, the ready made one is under the cummerbund.'

Gemma hands me the bow tie and I attach it under my collar. She settles back on the sofa, flicking the remote. I go into the bathroom to get a better idea of how I look.

'This will have to do.'

'I think you look really well.' She's generous.

'I hate the thought of this.'

'You always say that, only to have a really good night. Just go, be yourself, you don't have to impress anyone. Remember they aren't perfect, some have money, that only makes them spend more, most have problems, just as mortal as the rest of us!'

'I love you darlin.'

'I love you too, now bugger off!'

I grab my keys and wallet with the invite, I reach over the sofa and kiss her full on the lips.

The Ulster Reform Club, Royal Avenue Belfast

Saturday November 28th, 2009
Cropredy Reunion Dinner, 8pm.

Dennis takes my overcoat in the foyer, I sign the visitor's book and make my way past the Winston Churchill memento, up the staircase to the main reception room. The fire is lit and well catered for. A group of smartly dressed men with their backs to me jostle one another in familiar banter. I walk over to the turreted window alcove and gaze out at the throng of Christmas shoppers, delivery vans and buses, all oblivious to my presence. The rain is coming in sheets from Belfast Lough, exaggerating the twinkle of fairy lights in the panes.

'Donaghoe? Is that you?'

A bolt surges through me, breaking the spell, I can feel myself being reeled in, I offer my back to whoever it is for a little longer. They might regret shouting my name across the room and give up.

'Will Donaghoe you old bugger!'

I have no drink to hide behind, no comfort zone props, I turn and face the voice.

'It's Strangely Dark! Better known as Ainsley Park.'

'Ainsley,' I say tentatively.

The slot machine of remembering winds its arm back in my brain. I haven't a bloody clue who this is, however I smile and shake his hand vigorously, hoping it might jog my memory.

'You can still call me Strangely if you want.'

'Strangely, how are you?'

'Oh you know…so so, took a bit of a knock at the start of the year, but heh.. who didn't?'

'Indeed, it's been tough all over.'

'Can I get you another drink? You are running a bit low.'

'Yes, don't mind if I do, Ballentines with a dash.'

We both proceed to the bar; I am armed with a resolve not to humble myself by asking 'Strangely' how he remembered me. As we close in on the Members bar, the frenetic activity picks up a pace and slowly I begin to put pinched out features onto juvenile faces. Some of these people were friendly to me, some were bullies. For a moment I'm reminded of those old Dutch masters, where the town elders crane out to gaze at you from every space on the canvas. The heat and the interaction, the hubbub of an assembly roll call. It amazes me how many seem to behave like it's a re-run of 1985. The drinks appear and I toast 'Strangely'.

'Bones!'

I know that voice. 'Rawnsley!'

'What a turn out eh?'

'It's a credit to you Hugo, really!'

'Is that you Strangely Dark?'

'Yes Hugo, long time no see.'

'Shouldn't bloody wonder, never did like you!'

'I know Hugo.' he winces.

'Listen here,' I shout above the noise. 'Here's to us, there's none like us!'

'To us!'

We group hug in the manner expected at such occasions and Rawnsley pretends to shake 'Strangley' by the hand, only to thumb his nose at him with a wry smile. Moments later, the Master of Ceremonies appears.

'Ladies and Gentlemen of Cropredy Class of 1985. Please take your seats in the banqueting hall for supper.'

Rawnsley is in his element at the Top table. To his left and right he has former members of the Sixth Form Committee, the former Principal of the school is further down, with tonight's guest speaker, the historian, Ryman Rhama. Table settings follow rigid class set allocations, so I find myself sitting beside Tamara Horleck and Brent Drammer. We knew that we are captive to this, but we still signed up for it nonetheless. I guess we were trying to rekindle something that had long since gone out. Tamara tells me her story as I keep pouring, its hard to hear her over the din of toasts and laughter. She was a boarder, back in the day, half German by birth from a service family. It was quite cathartic really, listening to where we might have done this, if only I had tried that. Brent had gone into the family business; the more he spoke, the more I realized how affable he was, how he breezed through with little effort. He, like myself had a failed marriage under his belt, but he was enjoying the single life and he was able to throw more attention into the business.

The different courses ebb and flow and with it waistbands and tongues loosen. On numerous visits to the loo I decide to ensconce myself in a cubicle and listen to the urinal chat. How these people unravel, fuelled by alcohol and pent up inhibitions. Old bitchiness and rivalries rear their ribald heads after a quarter of a century, and that's just the men!

The night wears on and I make an effort to chat with those who mattered at the time, I nod to those who still don't. By 11pm the groups have crystalised into the cliques of old. The trendies, the rowers, the rugger buggers, the hockey socks, the nerds, the licks and the outsiders. The Master of Ceremonies appears again.

'At this juncture Ladies and Gentlemen, we have two choices. Dancing to be held next door in the company of the Riving Bunny or conversely, a night tour of the entries of Belfast with Resurgam Tours.'

Dominic Purcell 28, waits patiently at the Reform Club reception desk. This is his last tour party of a busy Saturday night and frankly it shows as he perches on Dennis's desk with his rain sodden cape and clipboard.

'How many are up there Dennis?'

'I have 150 signed in for the Cropredy dinner.'

'I wonder how many want to go out in the pissing damp after a slap up meal and then a dance with Riving Bunny?'

'Give me Riving Bunny any day!'

'You're serious Dennis aren't you?'

'I love their version of Hucklebuck, the way it melds into Reet Petite!'

'Well okay then, you should get someone to cover for you when they start playing that, so you can join the chain.'

'I was going to get Joyce to watch the desk later.'

Dominic sighs into himself and strokes his hair, the Grandfather clock by the cloak rack strikes 11.30.

'That's a wicked night now,' Dennis shrugs as he pulls the curtain strings on the entrance double doors. 'It's coming straight down in sheets!'

Dennis cranes an ear in the stairwell to hear if Riving Bunny have begun their set. Dominic dries off his itinerary, he can take up to twelve people with him, but smaller groups are easier to manage.

'You know I don't care if there are no takers tonight, this gig is prepaid anyway, Resurgam get their money.'

This was always a stopgap in Dominic's eyes. It took him long enough to realise that he wanted to act, having fallen in and out of retail and public sector positions since leaving Trinity with a first in English in 2001. Resurgam pay cash in hand, he can conduct three tours an evening in good weather and his employer, Mr. Unlive pretty much lets him get on with it.

'Are you the guide for the tour of the entries?'

'Yes I'm with Resurgam tours,' says Dominic. 'Can I take your name? Damn, my pen nib is damp! Dennis, have you got a spare pen?'

'Shh...try the left hand drawer, I think they are starting up.'

'Dennis is a fan of Riving Bunny. Your name is?'

'Will Donaghoe.'

The three of us stare up at the ornate light fitting which begins to gyrate to the rhythm of 'Do The Hucklebuck'.

'That's it I'm off upstairs, you two can mind the desk for a bit.'

'Cheers Dennis, what if I get a call from one of the members rooms?' asks Dominic.

'Press the green button on my desk for Joyce in housekeeping.'

With that Dennis springs up the stair rail and on into the Reception landing. No one rings and no one else signs up for the tour.

'Dominic I was wondering if you could take me to see Mr Unlive?'

'That's an unusual request,' he looks at the clock face, 11.45pm. 'I hardly know the man, he's very private don't you know.'

'Yes I'm sure he is, but he knows me and you work for him.'

'They are two different things entirely. Mr Unlive has been good to me, he saw me busking in the entries, he offered me this position.'

'I don't doubt his integrity, I would just like to meet him at a time of my own choosing.'

'Well this is most unusual, but seeing as this gig is a write off what with all the bad weather, I don't see any reason why I can't escort you to his home.'

Dominic rings the green button, after an interval Joyce appears.

'Has that old Ejit gone up there to make a spectacle of himself?'

'He said that I should ring you, no one has opted for the tour tonight so would you mind signing my job sheet Joyce?'

'Not at all young man, give me your pen. Now sir, can I get your coat for you?'

'Yes Joyce, here's my ticket.'

'Did you enjoy yourself this evening Mr...?'

'Donaghoe, yes I did, it was very interesting.'

'Sure it was great to catch up with so many faces you haven't seen for a kings age?'

'It was, Joyce. I must admit that I was dreading the thought of having to rake the coals of my past, but I think I came out of it rather well.'

'The grass isn't always greener on the other side Mr. Donaghoe, I'm sure you saw that tonight behind the facades.'

'I did, thank you Joyce. Are you ready Dominic?'

'Yes Mr. Donaghoe, it's not too far from here and I will try and shelter us both under this large umbrella.'

'Goodnight Gentlemen,' said Joyce. She folds back the door curtains as the rain pelts off the mosaic tiled floor draining from the red hand of Ulster.

The downpour is incessant and what is a short trip is staggered by the avoidance of large puddles along the way. We enter Joys Entry from High Street, the narrow dogleg that broods at any hour of the day. Half way down, McCracken's pub with steamed up windows and chants of 'Whiskey in the jar' bouncing off the walls as we pass by. A couple are entwined by the goods exit, they grapple each other in the drizzle. He bumps his head under a hanging basket, she pays no heed to the soil that collects in the folds of her blouse. Dominic looks at me and shrugs, we have all been there, passion loves opportunity. Further down we reach his doorway, it is just how I imagined it when I first dreamt him.

Dominic knocks twice, then once more. Bolts depress and slide on the other side of this reinforced doorframe; it comes ajar with a little effort.

'Dominic, so soon? I thought you had a late tour?'

'It was a wash out Mr Unlive, I have brought tonight's takings and I have here a gentleman who wishes to speak with you. I believe you have met before?'

He turns to me slowly and without hesitation says, 'Why Mr Donaghoe, won't you come in, both of you?'

'If I may just use your loo Sir, I will leave you the takings and be on my way, Karen wasn't expecting me home early and I can surprise her.'

'Very well Dominic, you know where the toilet is. Can I tempt you at this late hour Mr Donaghoe?'

'Why yes thanks, it will keep out the damp.'

'Indeed it will.'

'Thanks again Mr Unlive. I'll check my rota with you tomorrow if that is okay?'

'That's fine Dominic, safe home.'

He bolts the door and paces through the panelled hallway to the kitchen area where we sat before.

'I spend so much of my time in this room. I like to think of it as the heart of the house. The fire has the best draw here. The other rooms have high ceilings and are draughty, so I have covered their contents with dust sheets and locked them behind me.'

'Have you ever had any bother living here? It's a bit hard-by, what with the pub and pedestrians.'

'I have had my moments here, but I can take care of things should they arise. The pub as you know has been sold under a compulsory purchase order.'

He pours from the jug and reaches me a cup of sack.

'That was a foul evening to be out, my takings will be down judging by the cash box Dominic brought back. Still it brought you here Mr. Donaghoe.' I half smile as he raises his cup in my direction.

'Can you tell me more about yourself and the Americans?' I ask.

I take a sip of this wine I'm certain that I couldn't buy, even on-line.

'With Kingsevil oil comes great responsibility. I have altered my human condition by consuming it, I am free from pain and illness, while I have also witnessed swathes of others wither on the vine.'

'You say you have witnessed this, you have the ability to change fate?'

'God has that ability Mr Donaghoe, he experiences all, and is all, he makes a choice not to intervene, that is his will.'

'But you have this oil that if consumed, could help take away so much pain and suffering in the world.' He shakes his head as I say it.

'I have been witness to suffering, the wretched corruption of my parents bodies is but one of many. My poor fathers frustration as the numerous balms he prescribed where rendered powerless against what was assumed to have been an airborne contagion. His desperate efforts to lance the growths on my mother's skin. The transference of those lesions in due course to his own skin. All that time I waited for the signs on my flesh, unable to tend to my parents as they festered. I saw their corpses hurled onto a cart with the others, caked in lime for a mass grave. Why did my father not offer the oil to my mother? Did he not believe in the power of Kingsevil after all? Why was I spared? Was my blood immune? What was I going to do now?

At first I thought ability was something you were born with, I know now it is something you have to grab. Ability is the strength used in an opportunity, these are often seminal moments and one such opportunity came my way not long after the loss of my parents. We shared a grace and favour cottage within a row of such dwellings near the Palace of Whitehall. The rent was taken from service to the crown and the tenancy was for the lifetime of the royal appointment. My father's death ended the tenancy. I can remember scrubbing the red painted plague mark off the front door and wondering selfishly, how long can I still call this place my home? The King had a strong constitution and often took walks in St. James Park with his courtiers. It was while out walking with his spaniels he did notice me washing down the cottage door with vigour.

"My dear Sir, you will cause a fire with so much friction."

How prophetic his words were, as within a year this great city would fall foul of a conflagration of biblical proportions.

"Sire, I wish to banish the memory of an affliction."

"What do they call you?"

"Unlive Sire, Titus Unlive."

"Then you are the son of the late Claude Unlive, who was of great service to our court."

"I am Sire, I was his bound apprentice."

"We are well met Unlive, for we have need of new blood at court, you shall I hope continue the role of Apothecary in your late father's stead."

"I would deem it an honour Your Majesty."

"Then the morning hasn't been completely wasted," he smiled at his Private Secretary. "I shall expect you to present yourself to the Master of the Roles on the morrow. He will give you a set of keys to the study room your father used within the royal apartments. Good morning Mr Unlive."

"Thank you my gracious sovereign."

My relief was palpable, I watched as his robust personage strode through the muddy carriage tracks that led to Pall Mall, followed by his foppish entourage. I had shown my metal, the strength of character my late father had tried to instil in me since our escape from La Rochelle. I had also lied to the King. My father toiled with me to become his understudy, but my concentration was often found wanting. The exuberance of court life permeated through the network of people who dwelled at Whitehall.

This was only natural given that the previous regime had banned all sorts of gaiety, including maypoles, theatres and even the celebration of Christmas. The King's restoration coincided with the birth of my awareness of my body and my feelings it was trying to express. I was often distracted at my studies by the colourful processions of dandies and ladies only too eager to be accepted at court. I was reigned in by the soberness of my father's attitude to his primary role as Keeper of the Kingsevil. This was considered an honour akin to the role of the King's champion. I had no trouble taking in the sense of occasion imbued by my father's role. I revelled in the fact that he was at the Kings right hand in front of the clergy, the power brokers and the frail who sought comfort in the Kings touch. This was now to be my role, his son, he would have been dismayed at my lack of medicinal knowledge, but perhaps he would have approved of my solemnity at each service of Kingsevil. Amidst the obsequiousness that was mopped up by those who navigated the King's favour, the traditional roles held firm, especially if his majesty could make a saving here and there. He gave me the position, but he was no fool, he gave me a probationary wage to reflect my inexperience.

So imbued with the confidence that my position was secure I collected the keys for my father's study in the royal apartments. How typical of him to choose a chamber with such a modest outlook. His touch was everywhere within, down to the last detail on every labelled cobalt bottle. An island workbench, with my initials carved as a boy underneath, lead lined sinks that were plumbed with hollow wooden pipes. A series of cabinets lining the walls, ventilated and locked. At the far end a wallchart of feast days, with his handwriting detailing the allocation of the Kingsevil oil. Beside the chart, the copper jugs were stored on a rack and lastly, a strong box containing the oil.

'I have taken up too much of your time tonight Mr Donaghoe. In fairness you cannot even awaken from this conversation, as you paid call on me. I see sleep coming hard and fast in your eyes. I shall call you a taxi.'

'I am sorry if I seemed to fade on you,' I said. 'I lost track of the time, and you have only really started to tell me your story.'

'I told you before time is of comfort to me, I will share more with you at length.'

With that he left the room and rang a taxi firm who stressed that they are inundated and might be at least forty-five minutes.

'Then I will continue if you don't mind, for I want to share with you.'

'Not at all.' I texted Gemma to let her know that I will be home quite late.

'You asked me about the Americans. Their connection to all this will unravel; let me tell you more. It was not long after I had settled into my role that I began to adjust to the machinations and intrigue that fed the court of his late Majesty. The King believed in protocol, but he was no stuffed shirt, his exile after the Civil War taught him how to be personable and ingratiating to those of any class. You must remember that the old regime had melted down the symbols of monarchy, so that in many ways this new reign was a blank canvas. The King wanted to usher in an age of reconciliation between the rival factions that had done so much blood letting. He pardoned those that had fought against his father, but he showed no mercy to those who had signed his death warrant. Even the dead were dug up and exposed on a jib, if they had penned their name against his martyred father. The more I was involved with the King, the more I realised that he was a contradiction. He favoured new thinking, yet carried on the old tradition of Kingsevil. He married not for love, but for alliances and took many mistresses. He declared war on the Dutch, our nearest protestant ally, and was funded in this cause by Louis XIV, the sworn enemy of England. I realized he did these things out of financial necessity. The realm was bankrupt, Charles had spiralling debts accrued from promises made in exile. Furthermore at the start of his reign he tried to ingratiate himself with his nobles by granting monies and titles. The biggest contradiction of all was his faith.

A knock on my door brought with it Father John Huddleston. He was someone who I had watched from a distance. In theory he was the Benedictine priest who ministered to the Queen Mother, Henrietta Maria. In practice he was a conduit for the Papal States. He had saved the King's life after the battle of Worcester in 1651. Charles was smuggled into exile by those subjects of the Roman persuasion, whom Huddleston had contacted. Charles owed him a debt of gratitude beyond wealth; Huddleston tutored His Royal Highness abroad and to the delight of his mother, he became a titular Roman Catholic. This secret would have been seen as heresy in England, and it shows the strength of character the King had to bury his true faith behind the vestments of the Church of England.

Father Huddleston showed me every politeness, he had no idea of my lingering resentment for his persuasion, due to the maltreatment of my Huguenot parents in France by the Jesuit attack dogs. We both shared pleasantries, he showed a healthy interest in the significance of the oil. It crossed my mind that if things had been radically different, it would have been this priest administering the Kingsevil oil to the sick and the frail and not myself. Father Huddleston had chosen to study at the English College in Rome. The college had proved to be a hotbed of martyrdom, it was seen as the cradle of strident mission work. Unlike the new world, where the old faith had found new subjects, England was seen as a fallen heretic. The Jesuit order was zealous and held influence over the college, every priest from any brotherhood came under their scrutiny. Father Huddleston was an ideal candidate to gain favour and influence at the centre of England's realm. The Jesuits sought a way to sway the populace; they couldn't do it through the Government controlled printing presses so they would try the common touch. Reaching the people directly by way of the mystery and power of the Kingsevil oil. Catholic ministry, though not outlawed, was at that time heavily censured, many services were held in the open air. Symbols of Catholicism were banned, seen as idolatry by the puritan inheritance. It was ironic that Kingsevil emerged unscathed from the Commonwealth period, as it is strongly symbolic of the old faith. I knew Huddleston was sounding me out, testing my attachment. I could see his integrity, but because of my own travails, I could see that he was held a prisoner of conscience by the Jesuits. That morning I showed him the strongbox out of courtesy for his position at court, but I knew I had to be on my guard. I strengthened the measures in place for security, and I took more precautions when handling the sacred oil.'

Just then a loud horn reverberated down the entry from the junction of High Street.

'I believe that is your taxi Mr Donaghoe, I must bid you goodnight, thank you for coming to visit me at my home.'

5

Paul Rideout, Head of Overseas Development at Richelieu-Mazarin Holdings is at work early this Monday morning. His concerns over the continued delay with the Belfast purchase affected his weekend, ruined his golf swing and annoyed his wife's concentration at her Bridge drive. He decides to pay a visit to Jodi Penn's desk. She has yet to appear, it being only 8.25 a.m. He scans the post-it notes and scribbled reminders attached to her Mac. Traffic below is the usual frenetic mix of yellow cabs, DHL vans, stretch limos, buses and pedestrians. He can just make out the intricate atrium that covers Grand Central Station. The spew of suits that flows from its base into the man-made gloom that rises over mid-town Manhattan. His office upstairs reflects his status, a corner suite of course, with shimmering glimpse of the Chrysler Building.

'Good morning Mr Rideout.'

'Good morning Jodi, I hope you had a good weekend?'

'I went out with a few colleagues, Jazz club in Greenwich Village, Miles Davis tribute, nothing spectacular.'

Jodi hangs her jacket over her chair as Paul leans on her desk.

'It must be important for you to swim with the bottom feeders.' she asks in a coy, but confident way.

'It's the Senior Partners again Jodi, I need you to nail this new contact in Belfast.'

'I have opened discussions, I intend to speak with him today.' she said reassuringly.

'Good, come to me with anything you have so I can take it to them.'

'Of course.'

Paul glances at his watch then nods at Jodi.

That guy, honestly, can I not even get my coat off and he's there waiting at my desk. He really must be under pressure to mix with the minions. She opens the Mylagan & Love file. She can see the outline of the differing property acquisitions clearly in yellow, highlighted on the street map for that district of Belfast. Funny thing, she has been ticking off the acquisitions one by one for months in different parts of Ireland, but never noticed a pattern emerge before. Previously it was deconsecrated land, sometimes in rural areas with no hope of planning permission. It always struck her as strange to buy land at full market price with no prospect of building on it. It was also curious that a team of archaeologists would then be sent to scour each location. Belfast was different; the parcels of land were forming a pattern in the shape of a cross with a building in Joys Entry at its heart. To Jodi this is mere coincidence, convenient to look at, balanced, the way she likes it. She opens the thumbnail named Carew. Ryan had been thorough up until about a month ago when his reports dried up. Each property had been detailed by him, the owners, or lease holders checked and contacted.

Ryan was given free rein to write the cheques to sweeten the deals with any reluctant clients. So far this was a good arrangement; Ryan had the conversational skills, backed up by his position as a surveyor. He had given Jodi details of his last client and the condition of the property in Joys Entry. Ryan thought the owner could be made an offer he couldn't refuse. To that end Ryan had introduced himself to the owner, a Mr Unlive, he had tried to ingratiate himself and earn the man's trust. Ryan had surveyed the surrounding area, above and below ground on behalf of Mylagan & Love. Jodi was made aware of the system of tunnels running under these faraway streets that she was polite enough to show she cared about. They were found to be very old and had been modified over time by the Belfast Corporation to incorporate the sewage system. Ryan was particularly excited about one tunnel on the subterranean map, it appeared to skirt the cellar walls of Mr Unlive's property. Ryan's enthusiasm came out in his emailed accounts, which would sometimes be sent at very late hours. Too late in fact to be down tunnels, but hey, if that's what floats your boat, then Jodi didn't mind. These reports detailed conversations with Mr Unlive, who from what she could gather was very hospitable.

Ryan mentioned more than once that he couldn't refuse out of politeness the refreshments that Mr Unlive had on offer. It was all Ryan could do to try and bring the subject back around to selling no. 13 Joys Entry. So when did the cordiality begin to dry up, and with it any contact whatsoever from Ryan? Jodi knows it looks as if she dropped the ball, but it was an oversight. I'll ring that creep Donaghoe, but I need coffee and a cigarette first.

'Good afternoon Will, it's Jodi.'

'Jodi how's it going?'

She can tell that he's trying on a faint brogue with echoes of Barry Fitzgerald in the Quiet Man. Jodi is a movie buff with perfect recall, she is ready for this.

'Not too bad Will, I was wondering if you could keep me up to speed with the last of the Belfast acquisitions. I haven't heard from my contact Ryan Carew in nearly a month.'

'Jeez Jodi, Ryan Carew!'

'Yes, what about him?'

'C'mon love, haven't you heard?' his tone changed dramatically, colder, more northern to her ears.

'I thought he might be on leave or something like that.'

'He's on leave alright, he's dead!'

'My god that's awful! Ryan dead, I don't know what to say.'

'I know, how do you think I feel? I went to school with the guy and I didn't know until he was well in the ground!'

Jodi gathers herself, it's Donaghoe she's talking to, not a friend.

'That's very sad Will, but the deal goes on with or without him!'

'I know, I have taken up the slack in Ryan's absence. The way I see it we have two stumbling blocks. Firstly, the building has a preservation order listing, which means we can't do anything to the existing shell other than restore it. Secondly, I have met with the owner, he has lived there for more years than you can imagine, believe me, he is in no mind to sell or move.'

'That's really not an option Will, my people want the property come what may. Have you made this guy an offer?'

'Not yet exactly, he's such an affable bloke, you find yourself just listening to his stories most of the time when you are with him.'

'Come on Will, everyone has their price, it's a blank cheque.'

'It just hasn't come up yet, I can't see him moving, his people have owned this property for generations.'

'But you said yourself that it is in a bad way, he could start afresh somewhere new.'

'The place is a time warp, but it's brimming with shabby chic.'

'You don't need to sell it to me Will, just buy it for me.'

'I can hear a bit of pressure in your voice Jodi, I can appreciate that even from this distance, do you feel kind of hamstrung with your bosses?'

Jodi pauses, this is him trying to probe his bogman nose into her affairs.

'Thanks for your concern Will,' she raises her tone. 'As Princess Leia once said, "You are our only hope" she grinds out.

'Then I will ask him straight out next time I visit,' he says.

'Make it soon Will, I need to give these people answers, God knows why they have a thing about this wreck of a place, but they do and they pay us.'

'I will, I want to ask him about Ryan as well, I will get back to you soon.'

'Thanks Will, goodbye for now.'

Ryan Carew is dead and I didn't know. That sure was a curve ball I didn't see coming. Is there anything in his reports to point to this outcome? Come on girl, don't beat yourself up over it, Ryan knew what he was doing, if he risked his health then that was his fault. Still nothing is worth that, the guy seemed to love his job, he was so organized and together. I have to write this up for Paul. Carew's death will not sit well anywhere in this memo, but this is a business transaction when the dust has settled. Donaghoe maybe naïve, but he's all I have over there now to sort out this deadlock. I will try and put a positive spin on it so Paul can tell the Senior Partners that he is optimistic of a sale soon. If Ryan was ill, did no one try and stop him going into those tunnels? I can't take it in. His poor family.

'Will, you always end up snoring after being with that Unlive character? It must be the grog he keeps pouring down your neck! You even snore when you're dreaming him, what's that about? Does he offer you drink in your dreams?' Gemma asks.

'As a matter of fact,' I try to say.

'I don't want to hear, I mean we don't have the time. All I do know is that you woke me clattering about first thing, drenched and not a little pissed!'

'I'm sorry darlin,'

I try and appease her with a cuddle under the sheets, but she is having none of it.

'You know today is my mum's birthday and we are both going to turn up at hers looking like we spent the night in a departure lounge.'

'You look fine.'

She does, but I'm a crawler.

'No I don't, I fell asleep downstairs waiting for you so I still have last night's makeup on.'

'I swear you look great, go and see in the mirror, you'll get another day outta that makeup.'

With that she storms out of bed to the bathroom. I stretch to invade her warmth. She returns with the toothpaste glass full of water and throws it straight at me.

'Pig!' She shouts.

I lie with the pillow drying my face, essence of Arm & Hammer slowly draining down my cheeks. She locks the bathroom door and spends the next hour in there. Eventually I survey the room, my clothes in various states of abandonment. The tuxedo will need a pressing, I should have hung it last thing, but I was too busy trying not to fall over anything. My side of the room is a shambles, the lampshade is at a jaunty angle and the headboard has mint juice surprise draining slowly down it. I sit up with my legs on the floor, not quite ready. I hold my head in my hands as if I have been a victim of some violation. A quiet insecurity at once greets me; it takes the form of anxiety, probably deep-seated emotions venting themselves after my guarded behaviour at the School Reunion dinner. I have nothing to reproach myself for, I behaved better than most and I definitely left before any of them. Anyway, I probably won't see most of them again for another twenty-five years! Others were in worse shape than me, much earlier on, hiding their nervousness behind neat whiskey. I know the stages of this anxiety, slowly I'm trying to iron them out, you could even ask Gemma if she ever came out of that bathroom and she would have to agree. I have toned down the ribald actions of the rambling barfly. She has the high ground today, I was very late and I probably drank far too much, but it was the culmination of many things, revisiting excess for an evening. She will let me mull on it as she drives over to her parents' house in silence.

These family gatherings can be quite an ordeal. You know exactly what I mean. After all, you are in essence intruding on a ritual that has bonded a group of people for years. Then one day you are coerced into entering this crucible by your approval-seeking lover. This elongated scrum of relatives, who flit from room to room, sharing nods and knowing looks in your direction. Would you rather do a power point presentation to a room full of delegates? If you knew your subject matter, then the answer to that is easy. Give me that any day to the withering look I received from Gemma's Aunty Meg as I lit up at the dinner table for the first and only time. The professional spotlight, even if you fluff your lines and you end up repeating yourself, well it will pass. The personal spotlight, the potential in-laws, the studied inquiries, the unwritten ballet of the unanswered question, "What does she see in him?"

This moment may pass, but it is as if Gemma's family crew the largest tanker in the world sailing at a low rate of knots down Belfast Lough. The awkwardness of these occasions does not improve like a fine wine. I bring the ghosts of many things I would rather not discuss over a stranger's nest of tables. It does not help matters when the rich tea biscuit you are first offered breaks and disappears without trace into the polar shag hearth rug. Every eye wonders will you hunt for it? Will you ignore it? Will Gemma throw you a lifeline? The situation is retrievable and it's not like you just sat on the prize Chihuahua, snapping its spine in the process. Does any of this sound familiar to you?

Gemma's parents married young and like the background music that permeates every room, 'they made it through the rain' and raised four children. Gemma is the baby, the last to leave, she is her father's darling and I had my work cut out from the off. His name is Frank. He's chief mechanic at the public transport motor pool. He got a reputation as a maverick back in the seventies, after standing up to some would-be hijackers who boarded his bus and tried to ram it as a barricade on the lower Ormeau Road. It was a trainee coach that Frank had just spent all week overhauling and he wasn't about to hand it over lightly to a couple of scallys. Frank is phlegmatic about the whole thing, but his quiet reserve is dressed in a strength that I know not to mess with. Gemma prepared the ground for me by smoothing over any awkward moments when we first met and accentuating the things we might have in common. These turned out to be a fondness for Glentoran Football

Club and a penchant for AC/DC. Armed with these traits I knew that I would be given a fair hearing in Frank's house. His wife, Rosalind was kind to me from the off, I think she could see how happy Gemma was for the most part with me and despite the age difference, we gelled and that I obviously was infatuated with her daughter. Rosalind was 59 today and I found myself welcome and privileged to be part of that celebration.

1690

I had been in the service of Charles Stuart for twenty years, when in February of 1685 he did suffer his final illness caused by a bout of apoplexy brought on by excess at an orgy. His slow demise was witnessed by many, lest any rumour should arise about foul play. Those who were intimate, such as I, were oftentimes permitted to stand in his bed chamber near his councillors and witness his laboured breathing. His majesty could still be quite lucid and on that final morning he asked for the shutters of the room to be opened so that he might see the sun over the Thames for one last time. His wife broke down and begged him to forgive her for being barren. He held her close and begged her to forgive him for forsaking her with so many lovers. When the end drew near, we were ushered out of his presence into the long gallery. The King's brother, James Duke of York and Father Huddleston were privy to the King's last moments. From what I have gathered on good authority, the Duke of York entreated his brother that Huddleston was the man who had once saved His Majestie's life and that now he was here to save his soul. Charles II took the last rites of the Church of Rome and fell asleep for the final time.

So an era passed with the shadows under the door. It would be left for much cleverer people to sum up his reign, but if I may try and do it some service. His restoration brought continuity to a land ravaged by bitterness and hardship. He had none of the otherworldly detachment his late martyred father was so prone to. He had learnt in exile the ability to cultivate empathy, he nurtured loyalty through an honest humour that swayed people. He was wise to the fact that tradition was rooted in the fabric of the land, he played to his strengths and the populace loved him for that. He was emblematic of the aspirations of a nation to better itself, culturally and scientifically, to overcome the adversities of fire and pestilence. How well he seemed to be able to read the mood of his people, he was aware that he was flawed and did not flaunt these imperfections. He never embarrassed his wife in public, his coffers may have been bare, but his swagger matched that of his cousin Louis XIV. This man was a figurehead who lived and died in our gaze, all too aware of the fragility of his dynasty. On his death the crown would pass to his brother, to whom the King had said, 'You will lose three kingdoms within three years'. That morning in February, as the mist evaporated over a waking city, little did any of us know that life at court was to change forever.

James Stuart, the new king openly promoted Catholics to some of the highest offices in the land. He kept an army over subscribed with Irish commissioned officers in readiness at all times, something unheard of since the Civil War. James riled the establishment, if only he had an ounce of his late brother's dexterity, he might have yet kept his crown. The power brokers entreated the Prince of Orange to invade, they assured the Dutch that there would be little if any tears, or for that matter blood, shed for James. The Anglican clergy openly criticized the King, the court fragmented as many retreated to wait for the outcome from the comfort of their country seats. Even the King's own daughters betrayed their father's trust and soon left Whitehall with other powerful conspirators including the head of that standing army. Everyone waited for a Protestant wind to blow from the Netherlands and chase James II into exile for good.

It so happened that I was mopping the floor in my study room one morning. I had spilt a mixture which had made me sneeze and my face was covered in a luminous powder. A knock came at my door, leaving me just enough time to wipe my face and make a decent reply.

'Are you Mr Unlive?'

'Yes.' I replied.

'Titus Unlive?'

'The same.'

'My name is Bentinck, Hans Willem Bentinck. I am Lord Privy Seal to King William.'

This man before me was dressed in wealthy attire and had an earnest face with a strong Dutch accent.

'Please come in.'

I could see that he was cultivated and he bowed as he doffed his feathered hat and entered my chamber. I hastily wiped down the surface of a high stool with the cloth I had just wiped my face with. He was quite tall and had no trouble mounting a stool and settling at the workbench. He wore a long brown Periwig very much in the style favoured on the Continent. His coat was of velvet with brocade, peacock blue or Azure with silver piping on his arm cuffs. The coat buttons were ebony and contrasted with the interwoven lace and silk shirt around his neck. He carried a wooden cane made of blackthorn with a silver handle. He balanced a calf skin leather shoe with a high wooden heel on the brass bar that circled the base of my workbench. I could see his composure as he took in his surroundings and at length he addressed me.

'Mr Unlive, the King has instructed me to make an inventory of the different roles and departments within the Palace of Whitehall, with a view of making some economies therein. Your position as Apothecary is not under scrutiny, however your role as Keeper of the Kingsevil oil is no longer valid or required.'

It took me a moment to digest the last lines of what he had just said.

'The King does not require the oil any longer?' I asked.

'This new King has no truck with outmoded superstition. He views Kingsevil as a medieval hangover, out of keeping with modern science and philosophy. It reeks of heretical belief in the power of miracles.'

'But belief is the tenet that binds our faith. Belief that our Sovereign is the instrument of God on earth and can deliver relief from pain by way of his touch with oils.'

'Be that as it may Mr Unlive, the ritual has a Roman flavour which the new King is anxious to distance himself from. You will cease mixing this elixir forthwith and any surplus now in your care must be disposed of.'

The resolve he showed was palpable, the breaking of a five hundred year tradition meant less to him than the lives of the many traitors now rotting in the prison ships off the Isle of Dogs. This man was what you might recognise today as a number cruncher, he had been given a task to rationalise the court. He was foreign like my late father, but he had no room for sentiment. My father respected the traditions of this country and took up many of its values, this man came over in a bloodless coup, brimming with new ideas on the modern role of monarchy.

'Mr Unlive, as I mentioned your role as Apothecary is unchanged, indeed in due course your service will be appreciated as His Majesty sets about uniting his fractured realm. We will have need of you in the field tending to the wounded after the battles we are sure to face. To that end, I would like you to be prepared to expedite yourself at a moments notice from Whitehall and conjoin with His Majesty's army in service wherever that might be. Do you agree to the terms I have laid out before you this morning?'

I knew that he meant for me to mobilise myself, to decant my remedies and potions in readiness, for all the omens pointed to a sea journey to

Ireland. It was here that the late King's brother, the deposed Stuart, had landed in Kinsale with a rebel army backed by the French. Ireland was as familiar to me as the dark side of the moon. Yet the matter would be settled there,

'Sir I am grateful that his Royal Highness sees fit to engage me in the coming operations. I will endeavour to prove myself worthy in the field to our men. This appointment is tinged with sadness in that Kingsevil always played such a morale boosting exercise in time of need.'

'I assure you Mr Unlive this modern army has no need for the mystic properties of holy oils. They are composed of men from many Protestant nations, not just these isles. Their belief in themselves comes from discipline and training, they have honed these skills on the Parade ground and now they will be let loose on a god forsaken land.'

I almost feel sorry for the Irish I say into myself. His confident air swept any doubt from my mind as to the certainty of a Williamite victory. Mr Bentinck stood and shook my hand firmly, he looked around the room and seemed to take stock of its contents. He turned on his heel, a buckle caught the sunlight for a second and was gone. I was going to Ireland soon, my heart sank and then picked up a pace. The strongbox at the end of the room held within it at least a year's supply of the oil. I fortified my lack of courage at the prospect of this Irish adventure by pouring myself a cup of sack, to which I added to regulate my heart once again, a measure of Kingsevil oil.

My consumption of the oil began in earnest on my landing in Ireland. I brought every last drop with me contrary to Bentinck's instructions. I wagered correctly that the coming campaign would concentrate minds in other directions. I was brought up in the tradition that surrounded this ancient remedy which I deemed to be immune from the whims of a regime bent on change. The oil was for my personal use, it would fortify me and it might be of some service to the sick and the wounded in my care. I decanted it into kegs which were stored on racks within a covered wagon. This was to be my home for the next few months while on campaign, I had a driver and enough room to dispense and to sleep. This unfamiliar country with its sodden terrain, pitiful roads and unpredictable weather conspired against my constitution. How was the King's Apothecary to be taken seriously if he had no remedy for this bog trotters paradise? I diagnosed myself after the perilous sea journey to have grown a stone in the region of my kidney that caused me considerable discomfort and the passing of much water. This stone, which I admit I had been aware of but previously ignored, was now the size of a small round of grape shot. I upped my dosage of oil to compensate for the pain and found that I was able to continue with my work without relying on the crude surgery often required to remove the stone. I have always had a weak stomach and the damp conditions, mixed with regular upheaval and poor sanitation led to my falling foul to dysentery. This would have finished me off I am certain, but for my consumption of the oil, which restored my strength.

I was so preoccupied with my own condition that I remember little of the welcome we received on arrival in this country. The fleet witnessed bonfires on the hillsides adjacent to Belfast Lough, resplendent beacons heralding the King. The people lined the foreshore anxious to show their loyalty, our senior officers and the King's contingent were billeted in the homes of the good townsfolk of Carrickfergus. Our progression was often hindered in the most well-meaning way by those ardently loyal subjects of his Majesty. Belfast was well stocked and provided much needed stores and victuals for our polyglot army. Our stay saw the ranks swell with volunteers anxious to have a go at the Jacobite host. To the troops in my care I prescribed some remedies that would in reality only provide psychological respite from the real maladies that they assumed ailed them. For many it was uncertainty and homesickness, this had of course no cure other than a shoulder to lean on. I have found that the belief in a remedy can stir the mind to equip the body with enough strength to carry on, so I would often distribute among the men ampoules of coloured sugared water mixed with a little Kingsevil oil to be taken for anxiety or depression. It struck me that the anxiety our own men felt must have been twofold for the enemy. His army was also a mixture of nations, and morale and supply would have been stretched to the limit. Both factions had spies and were vulnerable to rumour and false propaganda. The journey south was proximate to the eastern seaboard in case we needed to be supplemented or even evacuated by our fleet, which shadowed our movement. Our military caravan stretched eighteen miles along the unmetaled roads of the Irish countryside. We made progress, but the enemy always appeared to be eating out on our arrival at any major town or ford in any river. Our men foraged as we progressed, the welcome further south was less than hospitable, but strict orders were observed not to pillage and to pay for what we required. The native Irish tolerated our presence, they bided their time, holding out for a Jacobite victory. Looting was punishable by death and the crime was meted out to the stragglers in our group at intervals along the route as a lesson to others.

I saw much privation among the inhabitants, understanding as I did that two large armies did so much behave like a plague of locusts on the land, leaving little for the natives to farm or to gather in. I also saw a belief in these people that touched me; they would congregate in the fields where there was no church. They took the body of the host in their mouths kneeling in bog meadows under the canopy of dripping trees. Their faith was undiminished and impressed me; it was honest and undiluted by wealth and status. The coming cataclysm would test many peoples faith, but what I saw in the fields of Ireland was the most pure undiluted belief I had ever seen. I must admit that I questioned my being there, my intrusion on this spectacle; I decided that my role was to help and to help anyone on either side who needed it. Before I started consuming the oil I would have been too wrapped up in my own predicament, what with the kidney pains and weakness brought on by too many stools. The damp climate in the middle of summer would have made me fret, the local customs which at first were alien to me, but on closer inspection were bonded in family and place. Gradually I began to realise that the Irish inhabitants were the real victims in all this states craft and politicking.

The clash, when it came, caught me completely off guard as my driver, Clarence Masham was away getting our dray horses re-shod. We had camped for the night parallel to a great and bending river. I woke to a cannonade, a crescendo of tapers and cloudbursts, which strafed what was thought to be the relative safety of our supply lines. I heard much commotion outside my canvas wagon, which was perched on two barrels that I prayed did not contain gunpowder. I knew that I was a sitting duck and that if the Lord called for me now I was ready. But none the less I decided to dress to meet him, I gathered my leggings and rolled them on, they had aired all night on the outside of the wagon. I stretched into my doublet, the numb pain of the stone in my side. I buttoned my breeches and ran a comb through my hair. I looked out and saw the vanguard of the King race in my direction. I barely had enough time to jump down from the wagon when they were upon me.

'Unlive the King has been grazed by a cannon shot!' cried his Adjutant, his horse shaking with sweat as it reared before me.

The King pulled on his rein with one arm and did sway somewhat on his bridle.

'This is nothing but a mere trifle Mr Unlive, but my people won't let me continue with this engagement until you cast an eye over the wound.'

I composed myself and reached into the cabinet under the wagon seat and took out my spectacles.

'Would you dismount Sire?' I said.

'Yes if you think it necessary.'

The King was attended to with much fuss and appeared out of a crowd of hangers on. He was resplendent if a little shaken and gun smoke had darkened his complexion. I could see a tear in his tunic near the shoulder above the blue Garter sash he wore. I asked him to take off his hat and if he could remove the tunic and the sash. This he did which encouraged me, and led me to believe the wound, if any, was superficial.

'Please sit Sire, let me unbutton your shirt and examine the wound.'

The King sat on another barrel in the centre of a circle of people. His servant did bring him a glass of wine, which he supped at intervals while asking his aides for the latest reports of the ensuing battle. As I pressed around the graze, he did look up at me nonchalantly.

'We are fortunate my Liege, it is but a flesh wound which I can treat with a cold compress. May I say that you probably made a target to relish for any enemy cannonade!'

'Quite so Mr Unlive, my people tell me to dress down, but I want to lead from the front and boost morale dressed as a King!'

'Then you will live to fight for this and many other days I hope Sire.'

With that I cleaned the wound and dressed it for him as best I could so that he would have a modicum of movement. I did not risk adding any oil to the ointment I rubbed into the King's light wound, Kingsevil has a distinctive smell, which he might recognise and I would have some explaining to do.

At length the vanguard escorted his Majesty back to his tent. He was to change his spattered and torn tunic while planning the next attacks. Clarence, my driver returned and was irked by the fact he had missed so much commotion. I was never one to brag, but my injured charges soon put him right as to the King's visit.

'That be typical Mr Unlive, typical. Him as close to thee as a coin in my hand and I was with the smithy!'

'He caught me out Masham, I hadn't even time to throw water around my face!'

'Well you be the one he came to in need, I hear he has a long memory, as long as his nose I reckon, he won't forget those who did good service.'

'I'm sure he has enough to think about Clarence. We had better boil up some more water and clean these poor fellows wounds.' I said.

'Right you be I reckon, they are coming in those that can, it's the one's that we can't reach out on the battlefield that I feel for. Those poor devils, lying there, calling for their mothers.' he said.

'That's enough Masham, no more talk of that nature in front of the wounded.'

The casualties mounted up as the day wore on, we snaked our way nearer the front as the battle burned on. Soon we were giving aid to rebels who had been caught up in the melee, our own men didn't begrudge this camaraderie of affliction. This was to be the longest day of my life, nothing quite captures the devastation, suffice to say that I saw men fall that only moments earlier did engage me in conversation. Their broken bodies, inanimate and hollow, their faces etched in pain, their last words uttered as they floundered in the river crossing. The brave men who faced such a hail of shot as they balanced their weapons above their heads to cross over to the other side. Their waterlogged clothing holding them down as they tried to dodge the bullets from the Jacobite sharp shooters on the far bank. The sheer numbers within our ranks did in actual fact create too many targets to aim at, and this resulted in our bridgehead at many points were the river was fordable. Once across our army began to have the upper hand. The enemy caused much havoc with daring cavalry charges which had no end product, save that of the death of the Duke of Schomberg. These charges were not supported by infantry and as far as I could tell, the rebels were in disarray as to what plan of action to enact next. The line had effectively broken and without King James in the field to bolster his men, many ran and regrouped at a hilltop near a place called Donore for the final reckoning. Many more ran on past that hill, down the Dublin road disgorging weapons and accoutrements as they fled. It was a story told by the fires that night that King James was the first person to reach Dublin to be able tell of his own defeat. So our King knew the value of being seen amongst the throng, despite the risks it was as good for morale as a regiment of fresh Dragoons. He did run close to death again that day, but his luck held and our army retained the field.

Of this I can confirm, nothing looks as bad as a battle lost, than perhaps the look of a battle won. Both have equal ingredients of suffering, both bring out the best and the worst angels of our nature. I saw severed limbs strewn in hedgerows, pools of blood along dirt tracks that led to bodies piled high for mass interments. Those who made it their business to shadow a great army did now prey on the dying as they breathed their last. They pocketed personal items from those unfortunates before they were even cold, tugging at rings on stiffening fingers. Wives and lovers, who had waited near our wagons for the outcome, had taken possession of the field in the evening gloom, calling for their loved ones. Dead horses were butchered were they had fallen, by those intent on having meat on the menu. The vanquished that lived were herded and drum rolled into an uncertain future. The victors gathered around bonfires with extra rations from a generous King. I made it my intention to live that night as if it were my last, for what I had seen that day had shocked me into living every moment. I wanted to be with a woman, for so stimulated was I that the need for an outlet for avarice was overwhelming. I did walk past the bonfires and take in the revelry, the carousing and bawdiness. The release was tangible in all others, they had outlived this day and it showed in their dancing and supping. The whores who did ply their trade to the army were busy this night, and I craved one to take back to my wagon. It was not long after making eye contact with a suitable wench, I did agree a price and also bought her a bottle of wine to sup as I took her back to my wagon. Masham usually slept underneath the axle and was nowhere to be seen at this hour. I took this loud, buxom woman and led her up and under the canvas covers. I lit candles as she stretched herself out on my mattress, I then uncorked the bottle and poured her a measure. She took it gladly and licked the rim of the cup suggestively. It was then that I perceived the matter, which caused me so much consternation, then and subsequently. I was unable to match her arousal with my own physically.

She sensed my hesitation and took it upon herself to initiate what would have been in the past second nature to me. Perhaps she took my indecision be shyness, and I let her as she stroked my breeches with her dirty feet. I love the proximity of women, the way they did carry themselves at court, it would often distract me from my studies with my father. I have always adored the way they preen and shimmer like fine porcelain, delicate facades to a passionate kiln. Oftentimes the Mistresses at court did call upon my father for aphrodisiacs to enhance their trysts.

They did flap around him and I'm sure he was flattered, I for my part hid my immature intentions beneath the workbench. Much later, when I was able to grasp the rules, I did flirt and often and I was fortunate to bed a number of ladies maids. I was careful not to fall for any of these girls, as discretion is everything in my work.

This craven woman writhing before me did warrant a good seeing to, after all I had paid for her affections. The seconds passed and I could see the frustration in her face as she fully expected me to react.

'Does not my Master like what he sees? Does he wish for me to undress him and take control?'

I want her badly at this juncture, she may smell of the stable, but I want her right now to my very core. My manhood has other ideas and I am unable to be of service.

'I will pay you extra for your trouble, it is quite a walk back to your part of the camp and I'm sure you won't get there unaided.'

'Have I displeased you? You did pay me much affection as well as money this evening.'

'Not at all, you please me very much, it is just with the day, the battle, the things I have seen here.' I try to paper over my failings, she could lay into me now, but no.

'I can listen too you know. Men talk to me afterwards as well!'

'I'm sure they do, it's just that I would have needed to know you a little bit better to impart what is going on in my mind.'

'Men want me to be so many things, before, during and after. You were kind to me, bought me some grog and treated me with respect, that is rare. The least I can do is listen to some of your problems.'

'I appreciate that, I mean it honestly, but you wouldn't believe me if I told you.' I ask her name.

'Peg Lane.' she says.

I kiss her, she reacts and fuels my thoughts, no reaction a midriff though and I unfurl the canvas curtain and bid her well. I'm left alone with the truth that the oil has stunted my libido, I look around and there's no cure.

The Americans

Thomond Babbage is the CEO of Babbage Pharmaceuticals. They have been operating out of Boston for four generations. Thomond is a first name long cherished by the family since their ancestors took refuge in the Thomond tower on the bridge over the river Shannon in Limerick. It was 1845 and arable land was under blight, tenant farmers were evicted from their homesteads if the rent was late. Landlords would destroy crofts and disperse families into the tender mercies of the

Many of these proud people were forced to beg at the famine w

the great estates. Many more died out of pride from not doir

The Babbages were fortunate to find shelter within the tower wi

other families. This tower had stood since the reign of King J

the thirteenth century and was once a Keep, a prison and now a i

It was here and in many other locations that Titus Unlive saw t

dispense his Kingsevil oil to the sick and the needy. Thomond Bal

grew up on stories of a man who remedied his ancestors, wh

no reward or merit, only that he was doing what he th

will. His distant relatives cherished the kindness an

oil they were given, which restored their health. The f

leave Ireland and seek new lives in America. Thomona

have Aplastic anaemia five years ago, he is now 60 and

what is termed a young man's disease. The irony is no

his pharmaceutical company have specialised in that f

of years. He has tried many different treatments from

new age and holistic. All without success, he retreats to

room every day losing his appetite for life. His family are close

often recounts the tale of the oil that restored his ancestor's health over the dinner table. His two sons, Dermot and Lyndon now handle the day-to-day affairs of the business. Thomond shares most things with his children since the death of his wife, but he knows that his new project would cause uproar with the boys.

He has a retainer with Richelieu-Mazarin Holdings, they are authorised to search and pursue any line of enquiry that might be linked to the widespread rumours of the existence of a miracle oil. This quest gives him a reason to believe he might one day leave the manicured confinement of his oxygen tent. He is a rational man, his wealth was honed through shrewd choices at a young age. This new venture is to say the least cavalier and his business head knows that he will be exploited, throwing good money after bad. His disability distances him from rational thought; his inability to be hands on leaves him open to the false hope generated by snake oil salesmen whose drink laden tales only lead up blind entries. Thomond knows all this, and he doesn't need his family to reiterate it and try to put him off, so he will keep it secret for as long as he can. Anyway the business can take it, they are cash rich and new opportunities for expansion are happening all the time. The money spent in Ireland will not be completely wasted as Babbage Pharmaceuticals can get a foothold into Europe with all the tax sweeteners it has to offer, it will be like coming home. The problem is the length of time it is taking to find any hard evidence about the existence of the oil. Thomond believes that he has established enough factual accounts from other famine sufferers at that time who owed their survival to a phlegmatic character who stayed just long enough to administer some medicine in the form of oil. There are too many for it not to be true, so who was this man who appeared and then disappeared again without trace? Thomond's business head kicks in to ask the question on his mind. Why did he not market this oil or drug? If it did what my ancestors swore, then it would have made him rich beyond his dreams.

What drove him underground? Was there some component that was seen as dark magic at the time? All Thomond really knows is that he is running out of time. Come next May, the end of the old tax year, the boys will want some serious explanations as to why so much money is being siphoned off into Ireland without any end product. More importantly, time is running out for him, for any quality of life he once had, to be able to play with his grandchildren, to watch them grow up. So far Richelieu-Mazarin have conducted inquiries across the breadth of Ireland, they have tapped into local history and regional rumour mongering, Parish records and census reports. Slowly a pattern did emerge, the stories of the oil always originated from areas associated with great poverty or hardship. The distribution pattern was by no means regular or widespread, often haphazard and convoluted. The results were always the same. After a short interval, the oil being imbibed, the recovery from whatever ailed the patient would take only a matter of days. By which time, of course, the benefactor had long since disappeared. It was not as if he even went from village to village, there seemed to be no method in his distribution. All that could be gleaned was that this person dispensed as he saw fit. Thomond decides to ring Paul Rideout at Richelieu-Mazarin.

'Paul, good morning, thank you for taking my call. Are we anywhere nearer to narrowing the search?'

'I have good news mixed with sadness.' Paul replies.

'Really? I'm intrigued, tell me more.'

'Well, I had a source in Belfast who was onto something. He was reliable and he was convinced he had found tangible evidence about the existence of the oil you are seeking. Trouble is he died before he could confirm it.'

'That's too bad Paul. The poor guy! Do you have anyone else who can take over the role?'

'Yes we have a realtor agent who has opened communications with the owner of the property we are interested in.'

'Good work Paul, tell your agent to make the owner a very generous offer, well above the market price, in cash if he wants it.'

'Yes Mr Babbage, I'll get right onto it.'

Paul decides to tell Jodi to her face, he leaves his corner office and decides not to take the elevator to Jodi's floor.

'Jodi, I'm glad I caught you. The matter in Belfast.'

'I'm working on it.' she says defensively.

'I know, but the stakes have been raised, tell your agent to offer the owner cash, over the market price in cash.'

'Yes sir, I'm right on it.'

Will Donaghoe had rung Resurgam tours earlier that morning and only got the answer machine, which sounded like Dominic's voice. He left a message asking to see Mr Unlive that day and whether it would be convenient. By 12.30 he had still heard nothing from Unlive, so he decided to go to lunch. Will long since cut the alcohol out of his lunch breaks and has even been known to bring his own sarnies, but he has grown addicted to the coffee at Café Anjou. It's worth queuing and if it's busy, then that's a good sign. Sometimes he can get a seat, other times he just walks back to the office with a takeaway. Orton and Sandra Morton both catch his eye as he puts on his jacket.

'Okay you two, who wants something brought back?'

'Can we join you?'

'Yes but I'm not treating you!'

'Rumour round here is you are made of money today,' says Orton dryly.

'Yeah…I just love spending other people's money.' Sandra quips.

'Nothing gets past you two does it?'

The three of them get a bench in Café Anjou. Orton has scrambled eggs on toast, Sandra has corn cob soup and Donaghoe has a panini as usual.

'Spandau Ballet have reformed and are releasing a single.' Sandra offers.

'They hate each other don't they?' Orton responds.

'Not as much as I hate them.' Donaghoe interjects.

'You said that with a little venom Will, do they hack you off that much?'

'The first time round I was sucked in by the aloof tartan look and I actually bought their first single. I think I bought their first album. It didn't sit well with me though, I mean Ian Curtis had just died and Bowie had just brought out Scary Monsters. So things were definitely in transition, I think Splendid Bollocks were a contrivance.'

'So you won't want any of their new stuff on the CD I always burn for you at Christmas then Will?' she asks.

'No thanks.'

'You remember Sally from Quell Dommage?' asks Orton.

'How could I forget him/her?'

'She's going to have the operation.' Orton makes a scissor snip action with his fingers.

'Are you trying to put me off my lunch entirely?' Will asks.

'Its just she took a shine to you. You haven't been back with me since.'

'Orton I know I can say just about anything to you, but flattered as I must be, Sally just doesn't rock my boat.'

'Sandra look how strong he gets when he is cornered!' sighs Orton.

'Come on Will, he's just taking the piss, I know how straight you are, I've caught you checking out my legs in the past.'

Will blushes a bit and Sandra smiles, thinking that it's sweet. Just then Will's mobile sounds.

'School boy error there, William.' says Orton.

Will shrugs and debates whether to answer, he looks at the caller number and recognises it as Resurgam from previously trying all morning. He answers it.

'Hello, Will Donaghoe speaking.'

'Will, it is Mr Unlive here, you seemed anxious to visit with me today.'

'Yes sir, I was wondering if you were free?'

'Of course my boy, how does three o'clock suit you at my house?'

'That will be fine, I look forward to seeing you later, goodbye.'

Will shrugs as they shake their heads at the table. Lunchtime is sacred time and mobiles are off limits normally.

'Is that the guy you are going to offer a case full of cash to?' asks Sandra.

'It is.'

'How about you and me just taking that case and heading for Acapulco? I can travel light, an overnight bag and some new stockings Will?'

'Sandra! You are totally making him blush now.' screams Orton.

Will smiles at Sandra, one of those I know that you were only joking, but if only smiles. Sandra nods unspokenly and looks away coyly. They drain their coffee cups and study their watches, just enough time to take a leisurely stroll back to the office. Will checks his emails and heads up to Gordon's office. This office functionary has prepared the ground, his desk is clear, but for an aluminium camera case containing £495,000 in £50 notes. It is twice the market value of Mr Unlive's house and probably the most cash Donaghoe is ever likely to see. Gordon was never one to see the levity of any situation as it only brought out the born worrier in him later on down the line.

'Just don't let the case out of your sight Will.'

Will knocks on Mr Unlive's door on the stroke of three. He remembered Dominic's distinctive knock that must be some kind of password. Moments later, Mr Unlive unbolts the door from the other side.

'Come in Mr Donaghoe, how are you today?'

'I'm fine sir, it is good of you to see me at such short notice.'

'Not at all, I got your message on that machine. I have only recently learnt how to play it back. Dominic takes care of all the technical things that I'm confronted with you know, he's a good boy.'

He shows Will through the dappled hallway to the kitchen where they have always sat. He notices a canary in the birdcage and he can't quite remember it awake or sleeping.

'Is the canary new?' he asks.

'Yes it was a gift from a grateful client, I still haven't got round to giving it a name yet.'

'It's very beautiful, and it sings for you?'

'Yes it is comforting, I won't offer you some sack, too early I think, how about some tea or coffee?'

'Tea would be nice thank you. White with one sugar.'

The stove is lit and he rests a whistle kettle on the hot plate and bids Will to sit.

'I see you have a silver case with you today - it's too big for a lunch box. Whatever can you have brought with you?'

'I have here an offer from my clients. I think you will find it very generous.'

'You said milk and one sugar didn't you?'

'Yes sir.'

He stood with his back to Will and spooned tea leaves from a wooden caddy into a tea pot.

'Perhaps you had better open the case then Will.'

Will got up and placed the case on the kitchen table. He fiddled with the combination and the latch opened smartly. He turned to Mr Unlive.

'I have been authorised to offer a cash sum of £495,00 for your property.'

'But Will, you know that my house is not on the market.'

'I understand it is a lot to take in, there is an awful lot of money sitting on your kitchen table.'

'No you don't understand, my house is not and never will be for sale.'

His appearance grew stern and he supported himself on the chimney breast as the kettle began to rattle on the hob. There was a palpable silence between the two men as each wondered what to say next without offending the other. The kettle began to sing and Mr Unlive took care not to burn himself. He poured the kettle into the tea pot which rested just above a Myson pot. He then collected two cups from the Welsh dresser and set them on the kitchen table.

'We will wait for the tea to draw Mr Donaghoe, I can sense your frustration with me. You are wondering why this old man can refuse such a generous offer. You look around you and you see my house with an agent's eyes, you see the distemper, smell the damp, the loose wiring, the rotten frames with mottled glazing. You think of the location, the proximity, again through the eyes of an agent. That cash can change everything in an instant and you can't for the life of you understand why I'm not biting your hand off right now to get it from you.'

'I forgot that you can read my thoughts as well sir.'

'I can't read all of them, just the ones that bulge out of your eyes. Why do you think I came into your life via your dreams? Do you not wonder why you and not someone else? Let me pour for you.'

Will is momentarily ashen and speechless. He let himself think that money could not be refused, as he would be forgiven for thinking until now.

Mr Unlive added milk and one sugar and gave Will the cup.

'I knew this would happen of course, but I thought if I made contact with you first by any means, then you would come to know my mind. I deluded myself somewhat into thinking that you knew your own mind and that you would be able to tell your employers that I wouldn't sell no matter what. Why do you think I have given you so much of my background? I was building up the level of trust between us. Did you not take in one iota of what I shared with you?'

His disappointment is tangible, Will is positively scolded and it doesn't look like he is finished yet.

'In your mind money solves everything, makes problems disappear. You make a lot less than you spend, so you are caught up in a vicious circle. You know the price of everything and the value of nothing. It's not your fault; you have been doing it for so long it has become second nature. Don't let your tea grow cold.'

They both sit as they have done before, only awkwardly. Will salves his dry mouth with a sip of Darjeeling and is bemused by the sight of all that cash on a rickety kitchen table.

'You were about to use the word sorry, and I won't have that. I decided to appear to you to try and change your attitude and to alter your thinking. I knew that anything I shared with you would be hard to take in, you lead a pressurised existence and I now how tiring my stories can be - that is why to begin with I would appear to you in your sleep. I wanted to try and help you see that you are harnessed to a yoke that revolves around money. Will did you honestly believe anything I have told you previously?'

'I wanted to believe everything. It's a lot to take in, the man pouring my tea has been boiling his kettle on that hob for the last two hundred odd years!'

'The kettle is only forty years old and I was actually born in 1645, but I get your point. My point, the one I really want to boil down to you, is this; I have learnt more about human nature than anyone ever who lived. I have seen disease, famine, war, torture, murder, ignorance and greed. The worst of these traits is most definitely greed. Even ignorance has no motive. Each one of the aforementioned has been manipulated by greed. The oil in my possession would fill this room with suitcases of the cash you so revere. In the wrong hands this oil would be exploited by the huge pharmaceutical corporations, the behemoths with gross turnovers bigger than the emerging nations in Africa. This sacred and anointed oil would be marketed, price hiked and labelled for worldwide distribution. Oil that formed a link between the Sovereign and the Lord would be available at your local pharmacy. In other hands the oil would be seen as a saviour of the church in whatever denomination it fell into. Falling church attendances would rise dramatically, congregations would clamour for the sacred cure that would be seen as the answer to all their prayers. Do you see where I'm coming from? Do you see the driving force behind this? Greed Mr Donaghoe. I imagine that you would receive a substantial commission for closing this deal? You could maybe trade in that Cinque Cinqco you drive for something that might encourage Gemma to settle for you? Before you take offence at these slights, remember, I sought you out first. I know you better than you know yourself. You are thinking that you don't have to sit here and take this abuse, but you do. You were tasked with this by people who think money can buy anything. The very people who pay you just enough and no more, so that you can't quite afford to make it out there on your own. Would it make you more comfortable if you knew you weren't the only one who fell into this trap? Do you think the Americans will stop trying to obtain the oil just because I refuse your case full of cash? Aah yes…the Americans! You ask me about them periodically. I have managed to stave off and stay one step ahead of various nefarious parties over the centuries who clung to the rumours of a restorative medicine. We both know it's real name. The people paying you are one of the largest pharmaceutical companies in the world. What do you think they want the oil for? Why are they buying up land at a rate of knots and doing archaeological digs? I asked Mr Carew the same question not two months ago when he sat where you are now. The poor fellow became quite obsessed with the whole thing. You know he died recently, you don't know what it was a result of. You only know what you were told by old school mates and colleagues. Ryan died from undiluted greed, shall I continue?'

Will leans forward, transfixed and defensive.

'Ryan knew his history, knew the prospect of tunnels under what was once the Chichester estate. These tunnels were not for defensive purposes. The grounds that surrounded the original castle in Belfast were landscaped to express a new era of confidence and once contained orchards and even a drive of pleached lime trees. Ryan had surveyed the estate for the developer before becoming entangled with Richelieu-Mazarin Holdings of New York. Formal gardens with box hedging were once laid out behind high walls, away from prying eyes. The installation of new irrigation methods using a system of underground tunnels enhanced the ornate fountains. High Street in the sixteenth century was the dock of the port of Belfast. Water for use in the gardens was diverted using gravity as a pump from a fast flowing stream called the Farset, which originally gave the city it's name, translated from the Irish. Ryan mapped the length and breadth of the tunnels. They were still passable up until the moment they were filled in by the developer. They were an invaluable source to ascertain the sophistication of the layout of the Chichester gardens and the whereabouts of the numerous fountains. Fountain Street is the only remnant above ground that we have to refer to today. He found a major tunnel that ran parallel with the cellar of my property. He knocked my door and introduced himself and his findings. I found Ryan to be diligent and engaging, he would visit me often as I said and we would share a cup of sack. I didn't choose to appear to him like I did with you and I enjoyed his like-minded visits. Ryan was a conservator at heart, he employed archaeologists to dig in the tunnels, even though he wasn't obliged to. I think he squirmed at the prospect of so much glass and chrome casing in such an old quarter of the city. His visits would get later and later, until I had to remind him of his wife and I fear he grew a little too partial to the sack I offered him. Sack as you may know is an unfortified sherry that is very much out of favour today, but is still possible to obtain through the right importer. Ryan would settle and impart all his worries into the early hours, he fretted about the lack of recognition he received from his employers, the lack of promotional prospects or the growing pains of his two young girls. I could see the change in his appearance. He grew pallid, tired and argumentative in a short period and for the life of me I couldn't think why. You asked me on a recent visit did I have much trouble living as I do hard by the public house and the busy thoroughfares. I have had my fair share of break-ins over the years, minor altercations with rogues who sought any silverware, artwork or other valuable items they could sell on quickly. You have seen my door bolts and you know the code to knock. My windows are barred at street level. You would be forgiven for thinking with my age and experience that I would be able to afford the latest security. It doesn't work that way. I was never able to splash out; it drew attention from the wrong people. People who, down the years would make it their business to try exploit me for the Kingsevil oil in my possession. So I definitely wasn't prepared for the late night visit Ryan paid me when I last saw him. At least I wasn't prepared to find him as I did after he had broken down the wall that divided the tunnel with my house. He had dismantled the damp and crumbling mortar by hand with the urgency of a madman. He wired up an arc light extension and searched my cellar until he found the barrels of oil. Ryan had rolled some barrels into the tunnels to take back with him and then for some reason or other he helped himself to concentrated Kingsevil oil. He tapped open a keg and must have been drinking it there for some hours until I was awoken by his rendition of the rousing speech before the Battle of Agincourt by Henry V. I could hear someone shouting and slurring two floors below me,

"Those men now abed in England will hold their manhoods cheap!" By the time I had risen and dressed, he was ranting in the corner of the cellar,

"We are but warriors for the working day!"

The oil was never meant to be drunk by the neck, it could be diluted and taken as a tincture, but never concentrated. Ryan had reversed any good the oil could have done him and his body couldn't compensate for the strength of the substance it was trying so hard to dissipate through his blood stream. He didn't even recognise me as I carried him back down the tunnels which were lined in sheets of tarpaulin to his portacabin within the developers compound. The night watchman missed me on his rounds as I called for an ambulance from the phone in his office.

It would have been too much for me to try and explain had I stayed with him. He was beyond anything I could have done, by ingesting so much of the elixir to prove fatal. I still don't know what drove him to such lengths. I felt awful that he was a guest in my house and that he was distracted by something that consumed him to such an extent. I would have shared the secrets of the oil with him, he was intelligent and sympathetic, but it was futile. I can only think that Ryan was driven to search for the oil by pressure from his senior partners. He must have scratched at the wall on his own for weeks in the damp and the dark before the mortar finally gave way.

You think me cold hearted, I can see it in your eyes, this detachment is brought on by the need for secrecy, which must surround the Kingsevil. It saved my life. I have used it sparingly over the centuries to save the lives of those most in need. It was never meant for mass consumption and it certainly wasn't intended as something you could buy over the counter. It was always my role as Keeper to protect it, Ryan was a victim.

I retrieved the barrels and patched up my cellar wall as best I could. Not long after the tunnels were filled in forever with foundations of poured concrete in preparation for the domed mall apartment complex. I read about the efforts made to try and revive Ryan and that they diagnosed anaemia. If any other explanation had emerged, then his family would have been under the spotlight at their most vulnerable. The company he worked for might have dragged their feet in paying out restitution to his loved ones under such scrutiny. I could do nothing for him. Your mind is racing Will, you even thought about going to the police with this just a moment ago. Believe me, after they had filed all the paperwork, they would still record a verdict of death by misadventure brought on by stress and that is even without the breaking and entering. I was the focus of all this, not the cause. Ryan was under pressure and it overtook him in the end.'

Will collects himself and snaps the suitcase shut.

'I don't know what to believe anymore.' he says.

'You need to contact your client and let them know that I'm not interested in selling at any price . It might help you work this out if you ask them the real reason they wanted to pay an inordinate sum for such a dilapidated building. Will, I know that you didn't tell them about the secret oil, they have been searching for it for years before you were involved. This goes right to the top, if you find anything out about their intentions, let me know.'

'I'm not sure if I want to speak with you ever again.' Will says solemnly.

'The anger you hold, that I left your school friend to die, it will subside and you will understand that I couldn't help him. I, with all that I know, simply couldn't save your friend.'

Will retrieves the case and looks at his watch, it is too late to return the money to the bank and so he decides to take it back to the office. Gordon is bound to be there and he can lock it up in the strong box overnight.

Will sits in his car after leaving Unlive's house in silence. The wipers turn in the twilight, the rush hour traffic never seemed quite so claustrophobic before.

6

Orton likes to talk, especially with a glass in his hand, Quell Dommage is a speaker's corner of sorts with a window seat down the Lisburn Road.

His coven are in full session and the subject of David/ Sally's decision to have the gender reassignment operation is never far from the surface. Sally was late arriving at the bar, she couldn't find a spot to park the transit van. She has been a Locksmith with Shevlins for twelve years and has so far managed to keep her orientation and well-guarded secret. The business operates from a warehouse in King Street, they employ eight at present, mostly family members and Sally was taken on as a trainee. The banter was turgid enough to implore her sensitive nature to pass her driving test as soon as practicable and allow her to work on her own. Her van has the usual masculine accoutrements expected with a Locksmith, portable key grinders, door and lock mongery, screws and compartments etc, very neatly organised. However she has modified the limited space with a set of blinds behind the key trays which allows her enough room to change into the lifestyle she really wants to express after work. Sally has wired up a magnified illuminated mirror to the back of the sliding door so that she can perfect the look. There is always a shrink wrap of Evian water and a family pack of hand wipes to clean off makeup along with a tub of moisturiser. She has an array of compact colours, eye pencils, heavy foundation, skin brushes and nail polish neatly attached to a purpose built shelf over the wheel arch. There is just enough space for a selection of size 10 heels on a customized shoe rack. She also has a choice of dresses on hangers under the ventilation outlet in the roof of the van and finally a drawer of different gauge denier stockings and underwear. She has perfected the art of emerging from the van with some poise and decorum. Sally is always conscious of the firm's reputation and would never drink and drive; she can always share a taxi if she scores, so no chance a cramped assignation within the confines of the van.

Orton likes to get the travails of his working day out of the way with a glass of his usual tipple. Sally responds by asking how Will is and Orton opens up a diatribe on how Will is now the 'bag man' for the mob, in that he had a suitcase full of cash to offer a client today. Orton was shocked that Will came back with a full case just as he was leaving the office. The client wouldn't budge and the cash went into their strong box.

'Same again everyone?' said Ina.

'Just a Coke for me.' replied Sally.

'A Coke, love? I know you're saving up but it's my round here!'

'I can't stay long, I have to leave the van back later as we are having a stock take tomorrow.' said Sally.

If I were callous, I would say that Gordon the office manager at Lydon & Dye didn't have a reason to go home at all. Gordon manages to shuffle enough paper after hours in that office to make the Police reticent to bother checking why the shutter is not down. Tonight is no exception, he has fretted so much over the large amount of cash they are keeping overnight. In theory he is meant to be calculating the end of month payroll, but other things keep cropping up as he wanders around the office. Gordon sees the devil in every detail and is oblivious to the grainy figure currently trying out different sets of keys on the front door via the security monitor. Gordon moves among the desks lifting catalogues and discarded paperwork; image is everything in this work, these young bloods on the front desks will never get another chance to make a first impression.

Sally left Quell Dommage earlier than anyone had expected and had changed back in the van, turning her overall with the company logo on it inside out. She had used Evian and hand wipes with moisturiser to take off her makeup. Sally estimated the different master keys she would need for shutters and commercial front doors as well as skeleton keys for the strongbox if necessary. She waited until 8pm and drove the van down one of those aspirational feeder avenues back onto the Lisburn Road. She passed by Lydon & Dye's offices. She turned back at the Kings Hall and did another drive by. The lights were still on and the shutters were not pulled over the front door. She parked opposite, just up from the bus stop along the park railings. The evening headlights glared in her face as she filed her nails and tried to fathom who was still in there at this hour. No cleaners at work, just one guy it seemed going from desk to desk lifting stuff. Sally grabbed her holdall, unzipped it and put on a pair of surgical gloves. She waited for the traffic to lull sufficiently and then crossed the street looking all the time into the front window beyond the display of homes she could never afford. The guy had gone in to the back somewhere as she was able to see right into the office showroom space with ease.

She pulled the shutters down behind her and jammed the floor bolt with a slim screwdriver. From the street you wouldn't notice, and it made it difficult for anyone to try and raise. Sally still had her back to the front doors and the monitor inside, she now crouched and reached once again into the holdall, pulling on over her head a set of 15 denier Pretty Polly smoky black nylon stockings. This was it and she knew it, the line had been crossed, something clicked inside and she knew instinctively which of her master keys to try on the upper and lower locks of the front door. Her heart began to beat in a way she hadn't felt since Lance had spread her open against the wall at the side of the Reichstag club some years ago. The front door snibbed open silently, Sally adjusted her stocking mask and entered, locking the door behind her. She was now at her most vulnerable, she could be viewed from any passer-by and watched by anyone within via the monitor. She ran the length of the showroom to the client suites, which were in semi darkness beyond. There were no cameras here and she caught her breath at a desk with a snow globe on it. She listened for anything to tell her where this guy was. Shortly after a muffled flush and a door closing told her that he had just been to the toilet, this was good news as he most certainly would not have gone to the loo if he had seen her on the monitor. Fuelled with this confidence she crept up the glass and chrome staircase and stood outside the room he was working in. At that moment Sally dropped her holdall and Gordon left his desk to check on the noise outside. He was about to lean over the railing when she clubbed him with her rubber torch. It must have hurt because Gordon hit the floor and Sally had to drag him back into his office and close the door. He wasn't sure how long he had been out for; it must have been quite some time judging by the knot work. Sally had long since perfected the art of rope bondage and Gordon was trussed on his stomach, just in his underpants, his legs strapped behind his head. Sally had gagged his mouth with another bdsm toy that was actually a leather mask with a ball choker.

'There's no point in you trying to struggle out of there, you know. I had plenty of time you see. I even had time to fold your clothes over there.' Gordon winces behind the gag and goes a deeper shade of red under the mask.

'Now I'm going to take this mask off you and you are going to talk to me okay? You are not going to shout or cause any mischief with me, are you? asks Sally.

Gordon shakes his head mask. Sally stands astride him and unfastens his mask and Gordon gulps down some extra air.

'You get used to the confinement in those masks quite quickly you know, it's part of their attraction. Anyway you probably know why I'm tying you up so intricately tonight.'

Sally sits at Gordon's desk, her overalls exaggerate her size in the mirror as she studies her outline in the stocking mask. Gordon is breathing more easily, he can sense no malice, but a confident intent from his interrogator.

'You know about the cash, it must be the money we have in there tonight. How do you know, who is working with you?' he asks.

'Honey I know more about you than you do, I know that you virtually live here every night of the week, not just because you are worrying about a safe full of cash, but because you wouldn't know what to do with yourself at home. I don't mean that to sound harsh, you have put enough extra hours in here to warrant yourself some of that cash in there.'

Gordon's head drops a little, he is belittled and bound up in his underpants on his office floor. This is where all that after-hours activity has got him, wait until head office find out that he contravened so many guidelines, not least that there should never be only one member of staff on the premises. That isn't even touching the insurance issues with such a high amount of cash and least of all the extra amount of electricity being burned needlessly. The red tape is as extensive as the binding Sally has so carefully arranged around his vulnerable body.

'Now you be a good boy and tell me where the keys to the safe are and I promise I will make it look like you were under coercion to help me.'

Gordon thinks for a moment and decides he is not the hero type, and if he was what good would that do him now?

'Second drawer down on the right of my desk. You will find the key for the drawer in my jacket pocket hanging up over there.'

Sally strolls over to the coat rack and feels through Gordon's jacket. She turns the smallest key on the chain in the drawer and it opens. The drawer contains a framed picture of a woman in black and white, two marker pens, a bar of Cadburys milk chocolate and a large safe key.

'You mean you actually keep a safe key in this drawer? It's the first place people would look!'

'Look again, under the chocolate.' he says.

There was a box of Vesta matches which rattled as Sally lifted them.
'What's in here then?'

Some dead head matches, three drawing pins, a chain of paperclips and a small key that Sally knew to be for a filing cabinet.

Sally set the key down and lifted the chocolate. She broke a segment and offered a piece to Gordon. He wasn't going to, but he opened his mouth and took the chocolate. Sally broke another bit off and sat on the table crunching it.

'So this file key opens a cabinet which contains the safe key? The large key there is just a decoy?' Gordon nodded.

Sally walked over to the row of filing cabinets and looked at Gordon.
'It's the third cabinet down, second row in.' he says.

She turns the key in the cabinet sweetly and retrieves a dead bolt key.
'Thank you. Who's the woman in the photo by the way?'

'She was my mother,' he offers.

'Is she dead?'

'She left when I was very young and I was only recently given that picture and I don't know if I want to keep it or not.' he says.

'I'm sorry, I mean it, I feel bad about this, but I need the money. Not all of it you understand, just some of it. Enough to get me through some difficult times ahead.'

'You probably shouldn't tell me anymore, that whole hostage privilege thing.' says Gordon.

'I know, I blab my mouth off, where is the safe by the way?'

Gordon directs Sally across the hall to the server room. This room needs a combination, so Sally tells Gordon that she will need to smack his face to make it look like she had to force it out of him. He understands and Sally slaps him repeatedly with her gloves. His face is suitably swollen and Sally was almost tempted to stroke his head in sympathy. She stands over Gordon and watches the monitor above his desk. Nothing but evening revellers and intermittent night buses.

'I will need to take the monitor discs with me too.'

She leans in closer as her mask blurs things a bit to try and find the eject button on the monitor, the disc pops out neatly and she pockets it in her overalls. Armed with the combination Sally enters the server room and is at once overpowered by the chill that comes out of there. She reaches for the temperature control gauge and brings it up to 18 degrees. The safe is at the end of a very small room, lined with terminals all clicking away.

'I have beaten your face enough for it to look convincing, I know that this whole thing isn't going to go easy for you. The cops are bound to think this was an inside job, but you are pearly white. The hours you put in, they show how much this place means to you, the money is insured, does that ease your guilt a little by helping me? Nobody expects you to be a hero with someone else's money, just tell me the safe combination and I will be out of your hair in no time.'

Gordon rests his head on the carpet tiles and calls out the combination.

'77, 78, 83, 92.'

Sally turns first clockwise, then the next anti-clockwise and so on. She inserts the safe key and the handle gives way and opens.

'My god,' she cries.

Amid the title deeds and documents, petty cash and sundries, a silver case sits on a shelf by itself.

'This looks like my ticket outta here!'

'It is, I didn't have time to create a combination on the case, so you should be able to snap it open.'

Sally reaches in and takes out the silver briefcase, she lays it on the floor and looks out across the hall at Gordon in the other room.

'Nice underpants by the way!' She giggles loudly in the rush of seeing so much cash. She takes £100,000 in crisp paper sleeved bundles and places them in the holdall. She could have taken more, but this is what she estimated would cover the operation and help her to start a new life somewhere else. She was on her own now, with no escape plan, how far did she think she would get? Everything had happened so quickly, she went back into Gordon's office, gave him fair warning, then knocked him out again with the rubber torch.

The fallout from the robbery touched everyone, not least Orton who at first revelled in the scandal and the scrutiny. As the nature of the crime altered and began to unravel and suspicions of an inside job were aroused, Orton was not slow to realise he may have indirectly been an accessory after the fact. He went on the sick before he could be suspended and continued to help the police with their enquiries from home. The penny really dropped for him when Ina called to say that Sally hadn't showed for work for days and wasn't answering her phone. Sally, who was always so punctual and never took a day off work sick. Sally who had set a side so much of her pay each month to go not towards a pension, but for the gender reassignment operation she so desperately wanted. Orton soon realised it was Sally who answered the androgynous description given by Gordon. She had been drinking Coke that evening, which Orton found strange, but he now knew it was to keep her sharp. She had made some half-baked excuse about a stock take, Sally had the skills and the motive, and now she had gone missing with 100k.

Gordon was forced to take some of the leave he was amassing. Any other employee would have been dismissed immediately, but it says something about his durability that he was kept on. He was discovered by the cleaner the next morning. Sally had bound him good and proper to his desk with intricate rope work that impressed the scene of crime experts. Gordon, importantly, was believed. The humiliation he underwent was too real to be contrived. He knew that the company policy was to cooperate with robbers, so as to limit risk and personal injury. The money after all was insured and the question most on police minds was why the burglar didn't take the full amount. Gordon told them that he was not threatened and that he thought his captor just wanted a sum that would help him through something difficult. His description of the burglar was spurious at best. The stocking mask didn't give away much about his assailant's appearance, a conflicting account of a man with equal amounts of controlled strength and sensitivity, enough of a contradiction to hinder the police for a time with an accurate identity. The breakthrough they were certain of lay with Orton, who as the days went by grew more isolated and insecure with the knowledge that his friend had used his information to jeopardize his career. Orton told the police about his suspicions regarding Sally, who by this time was on the Continent constructing a new sexual identity.

Will Donaghoe looked on all this with a curious detachment, he was dismissed early on as a suspect as he was considered, like Gordon, to be too close to the money to actually steal any of it successfully. Whoever it was, Will thought they had some balls, and the irony of those words are not lost on us. The office was a crime scene and the staff where farmed out to other branches for a few days. Will was allowed to operate his client list from home. He thought long and hard about Mr Unlive's one-way conversation. He had done a colour wheel of emotions regarding that man. His dreams had long since dried up, but his words hung in his mind with so many other unanswered questions for days after the crime had happened. The robbery was just a sideshow of the big show. Unlive had revealed his cold nature, but Unlive was no ordinary man. Recent events had quickened Will's sobriety, he worked from home and he tended to want to stay at home too. He was beginning to like it, he could pace out the day, plan and prepare proper meals that Gemma would appreciate, sit longer and listen to how her day went. A part of him even wished that Gordon might get something from his extended leave, a realisation that the office was just a means to all and not the end all that previously had demanded so much of his time. Poor Gordon the old retainer, trussed and bound, a poster boy of derision for the faceless number crunchers at head office. Was there anyway back for him?

'Jodi, good morning, it's Will Donaghoe at Lydon & Dye.'

Jodi waited for the sarcastic brogue and it didn't arrive.

'Morning Will, thanks for ringing me so promptly.'

'Jodi, the Belfast deal is all but dead in the water, the owner is simply adamant that they won't sell up. My feeling is that he suspects an ulterior motive to have been offered such a generous cash incentive. What with one thing or another happening over here, I have only now been able to cobble together some kind of compromise, so if you don't mind I would like to pitch it to you, as you might say over there.'

'Anything is welcome that would get me out of this hole Will.'

'I think your client needs to come out of the shadows and show an earnest intent. The owner of the dwelling here is aware that an American pharmaceutical company is purchasing property in Ireland at inflated prices. He also knows that your clients are just sitting on the land and not creating jobs or accruing any income from rent. Perhaps if someone from the company was to meet with the owner and assure him, then he possibly might be more amenable. I have exhausted the relationship I developed with him and feel that direct communication is the last resort. If your people are up for this then I could try and arrange a meeting with the owner.'

'Will, I totally agree,' she actually means it.

'I will pass this information on to my boss who will speak to the company about this. Your client knows more than I do about some pharmaceutical company wanting his property. Where does he get his information from?'

'He has been around for a while and has many sources, he knew all about this before I even offered him a case full of cash.'

'Well okay then, there is a glimmer, so if we can arrange a meeting between the two then something might come out of it?' she asks.

'Who knows, but it gets you and me out of a hole as you said earlier. Jodi I'm working from home for the next while and my landline number is 02890624183, you have my mobile of course.'

'Thanks for that Will, it's something to work toward at least, goodbye.'

1691

On September 3rd 1691 Titus Unlive turned 46 years old. An event he chose not to share with anyone. Birthdays, he knew were now to be consigned with any thoughts of mortality to the dunghill of memory.

For what good is observing a date on a calendar that millions of other strangers share coincidentally, without the love of a parent, or a child or for that matter, a lover to share it with. All these traits now belonged to Titus, he would adjust and grow wiser, without ever growing a day older. He pondered on the impotent loneliness that stretched before him as he penned his resignation from the service of his King. Ireland, he was naïve to believe, had suffered enough, maybe he could do some good by staying here. He was driven to drink the oil as a respite from the pains his body was experiencing, so why should he not now help those here who needed it most? His servant, Masham was right after all, King William did have a memory as long as his nose and replied to Unlive's resignation letter. He remembered what service Unlive had been and consented to pay him a reasonable pension for the duration of his life. Titus paid Masham for the wagon and two drays; they had shared in the bounty of a conquering army and grown close. Masham had family and reluctantly decided that he couldn't stay any longer than was necessary in Ireland.

'What will you do now Mr Unlive?' he asked.

'I am fortunate Clarence, I can make it my business to see after the needs of others. The court has no need of me. Anyway I'm tired of the falseness there, the biting at the heels just to receive a few scraps from the King's table. I can leave that to the next crop of fops and dandies.'

Unlive knew that his decision to stay was tempered with the knowledge and the sadness that he had closed the door on the life he was brought up in.

'This damp country must have got to thee I reckon, and you with all those mixtures up there on racks. Is there nothing you can take to ease your humour to change your mind and come back to England?'

'England will manage without me Masham, you have a wife there, children who need a father, it's different for you. I am a free agent now and the small pension will tide me through. I want to travel through Ireland, perhaps to be of some use, to bandage some of the wounds our people have inflicted on the innocent and the weak.'

'Then you are a better man than me Mr Unlive. For all I have done since I came to this heathen land is take my fill. I have not been proud of my actions while here, but I have learnt a little about human suffering and that was from watching you help the wounded. The men in our company respect you for it, your diligence and care, it saw them through the hard campaigns in the west.'

'I could have no finer epitaph, the plaudits of a commander ring hollow compared with you Masham. You have the ears of the troopers, the brave boys who slept rough in the fields and those who kept watch around our wagon on so many nights. They created this victory, but if we all leave then what will have it been for? Two crowns fighting it out over bog land far from any court. I want to make a small reparation, ease some of the scars we didn't intend to open.'

'Very well then, I can see you are thick with that emotion Sir. The boys will miss you come final muster, and for my part I was ever so glad to be in the company of so caring a gentleman as yourself Mr Unlive.'

'Clarence I have had some low times in this strange country, there is little here to remind me of home. A sheltered valley here and there, unscathed by skirmishes, perhaps did remind me of the home-counties, but in the main this is a foreign land with different methods. Your company was not chosen, we were thrown together, but we got on. The victors will soon return home with the spoils and the vanquished will pour back into France to lick their pride, so I have decided to stay here and help heal the wounds on this broken land.'

'You know what's best Sir. I have no doubt you will make a difference to those you wish to help. It has been my honour to serve with you and I would consider it a privilege if you ever a paid my family a visit back home in Wessex.'

Clarence Masham, a proud man, shook Titus firmly by the hand and they parted for the last time.

This was to be no easy ride for Unlive. Ireland was a cloth steeped in resentment and long memories. He had witnessed fervour here like no other, true faith that had moved him, faith that had long since been quenched under the bawdy coat tails of the Stuart regime. It was this faith that persuaded him that the people genuinely needed his aid. Ireland was always seen as the back door to England by those who wished to exploit it. Once that usefulness was consumed, the country reverted back to being a dormitory province that would be supplanted with colonists in the English model. Unlive stood out like a square in a round peg, the consummate example of the exploitative foreigner. This visage would be hard to shake or hide, how could a man hope to offer help, if those to whom he wished to aid did resent his very presence? The answer was simple, don't offer the oil to anyone, don't fuss, don't linger.

Travel the country, change route and direction often so as not to pick up a retinue or reputation. Don't create waves, don't be ostentatious, don't promote the oil to crowds or distribute it on a Sunday. Don't drink in hostelries, don't form friendships that could be exploited, don't ask for favours, don't give lifts to waifs or strays. Don't stay too long in the one place, even if it is only a sheltered spot. The land always belongs to someone and the word will get around about your presence on it soon enough. Don't travel at night lest you lose your way and be accosted by highwaymen. Don't talk to priests or ministers any more than you have to, they hold great sway over their flocks and can often ferment their superstitions. Don't take up the offers of hospitality from those gentry who are free with you. Their dining tables are hotbeds of gossip and the claret they pour down your neck will only loosen your tongue about the oil in your possession. Don't fall in love as you know only too well that it cannot be consummated, even if truly felt. Don't tip too much to blacksmiths or wheel rights as they pass on information to others that there is a wealthy stranger travelling alone. Don't visit the same borough or county twice in the same quarter as it draws attention and a regular pattern is easily formed. Don't presume that someone needs your help, this is the most difficult of all and can get you into the most trouble.

Armed with these precautions, Mr Unlive proceeded to traverse the island at a pace that wouldn't arouse attention, in a covered wagon that had seen better days, with two aging horses. The army had taught him how to set a fire and cook victuals for himself, he knew how to skin a rabbit, if he saw one he could catch. He fished in the many lustrous rivers and caught salmon bigger than he could eat at one sitting. He had grown used to the climate, the damp starts, the chill in the evenings. The loneliness was the thing that really got to him and he knew that it was something that he had better get used to. He read late into the night, passages by Milton, Locke's poetry, the martyred King's Eikon Basilike, books that he had obtained from Whitehall, before a fire consumed its gallery. These books were now a comfort to him even though they were sun bleached and ragged at the edges. He studied philosophy under canvas and candlelight, hermetic thought and pamphlets by Newton and Bacon. Now with such time on his hands he could study flora, gather wild herbs by the wayside and dry them to discover their medicinal values. He realised the gift he had obtained had granted him the time to devour knowledge, to better himself, be the consummate academic his father had tried in vain to nurture. He could now spare concentration on subjects that were previously anathema to him. He would chuckle to himself as he held the reins on some unpaved track that led nowhere in particular, it was not the destination that mattered he soon realized so much as the journey there. On the way, the many shrines to different saints always impressed him, often they led to a waterfall or holy well where he could refresh the horses without the need to fall back on local knowledge at a hostelry. These shrines would often have implored messages tied on ribbons to the branches of nearby trees to prevail and protect over the needs and prayers of different families.

On a particular morning, a weekday, Unlive stopped at a waterfall near a pilgrim path. A young woman in a shawl sat with her back to the path on a clump of weeds. He could just make out that she had a very young child in her arms, wrapped again in similar garb. Unlive stepped down from the wagon and fetched a pale from the side.

'Good morning,' he said cheerfully enough.

She still sat with her back to him, swaying slowly in the chill air.

'Are you well Madam?' he asked.

No answer from the figure huddled up on the bank. Unlive continued on to the waterfall and made the sign of the cross as he passed a large crucifix nearby and proceeded to dip the pale into the vibrant water. When full to the brim he carried it back to the drays.

Unlive stroked their manes as they slurped the water. He produced two carrots from a satchel hooked over the driving seat. The figure in the shawl stretched out a hand just as he was about to give a carrot to the nearest horse.

'You would like some of this? Why surely so.' He walked over to the woman and gave her the carrot. She grabbed it off him and devoured it, then as she munched on it she would mouth some it into her baby's mouth.

'My God,' he said into himself. 'Please let me help!' he said out loud. She muttered something in Irish and made to leave. He opened his palms in a manner that must have reassured her, for she sat again, or maybe she was just too weak to move. Unlive could see her pitiful condition, so he gestured that she come over to the wagon for some warmth at least. She threw down the root stub of the carrot, all that was left and carried her child over to the wagon. He helped her up the steps and she collapsed in a heap within. He covered her with some army issue blankets and she was soon asleep with her tiny charge clutched firmly in her arms.

'Please don't be alarmed,' he said softly as the girl stirred.

Night had fallen and Unlive was loath to move the wagon too far from where he had met the woman. But he must, for fear of night prowlers in such a vulnerable location. He drove the wagon through a glen below the pilgrim path and kept roughly parallel with it by way of undulating fields. He found a spot that offered cover and protection from the prevailing winds. This would have to do for the night, he would be careful to light the stove in the wagon, opening the vent slowly to let out the smoke. The Irish girl watched his every move from the relative comfort of the corner of the wagon, he could see uncertainty mixed with need in her eyes. The child she carried slept too much for his liking. The stove took and fumes dispersed, drawing heat from the wood he had dried.

'What is your name?' he asked her gently.

She had piercing green eyes which looked all the more bejewelled on such a dirt ridden face. He thought she wouldn't answer so he turned to attend to the stove.

'Gaile...my name is Gaile, and this is my girl Niamh.'

Unlive poured over the names in his head, the sound of her dialect, any sound, company, the child she carried, as the wind closed in outside.

'Gaile I hope you slept soundly. You must have been tired as it is now past nine. Do you have people in the area?'

'I have a brother in the army, who I haven't heard from in months, my father is dead and my mother takes a drink and could be anywhere.'

Unlive was shocked at the thought of this girl being reliant on the charity of strangers. This is what he signed up for when he undertook this role he knew, but the privations she must have gone through humbled him and he was angry that he had time to feel sorry for himself for being alone.

'What is the name of your village or town and I can take you back there in the morning?'

'Beal na mblath, it's on the road to Bandon.' she said.

'Gaile you must trust me now, I am an apothecary, the child you carry does not look well and has not moved since I met you. Can I inspect her to see if I can help in any way?'

'She sleeps a lot, the poor thing, I can get no heat into her.' she replied.

Unlive senses that he has made a connection and allows himself to take a step closer to his charges. The child was cradled with its face away from him and was too still for comfort. Unlive turned to Gaile's side and looked at the bundle over her shoulder. She had been dead for some time.

'Gaile I am more concerned about you than Niamh, she is with the angels now and no more harm can come to her. But you need to let go of her, so that you can grieve.'

'Niamh is all that I have, my brother stopped sending us money and we couldn't afford the rent. She kept me sane in all this turbulence.'

'I understand, but you have to think of your failing health, I don't think that you would have lasted much longer out there. I am going to prepare some lentils and vegetables in a broth and when the time comes will you share some with me?'

Gaile nodded slowly, she relaxed her grip on the tiny body and placed it on her lap. As the wagon began to heat up, her mind gathered up the last moments she had shared, she began to cry uncontrollably and Unlive tended to the broth, hoping she gained comfort enough from her environment to let out her grief. They would share a meal later, she let Unlive examine the corpse and it was malnutrition, combined with exposure that had done for the poor creature. Gaile fell asleep shortly afterwards and Unlive watched over her, as she would need all her strength for the morning.

How cold a room under canvas can get at this time of year he thought? The gap in the folds betrayed an inky sky with what looked like the hook of some constellation trying to peek into the tent. Further outside, not far down the glen, two conjoined foxes cried out in the night. Unlive needed little sleep now since taking the oil regularly, he consumed it with a cup of sack after his meal every evening. Life must go on he thought, even for this young woman with a dead child at her side, somehow she will get through this. He would fortify her in the morning with some mulled spices and mix in a measure of Kingsevil oil. He never wished for morning so much, not for himself, but for Gaile to have closure.

Before dawn he rose and took a shovel back to a waterfall near the shrine and dug a discrete hole at the base of a tree strung in ribbons. He thought it a suitable place as so many people came here to pray. So surely some of that fervour would trickle down into the remnants of her baby. It was only fitting to bury a small child amidst the aura and protection of so much devotion.

Gaile was awake when he came back, he bid her good morning and poured her a basin of hot water, gave her soap and a muslin cloth so that she might wash herself. Her flaxen red hair which had obviously been left uncut for some time, now swept over her face and into the basin. This act was a distraction for her, how often he had seen the process of grieving masked by chores, a pre-curser to going through the motions.

She like Unlive was now alone, this realisation would seep in with the hot water, the release, the insecurity. Titus gave her a fresh jug topped up with warm water and she poured it over the soapy lather in her hair as the basin filled. He didn't wish to stare, but the water draining from her accentuated her face, giving her more definition and led him to believe that she was still in her teens. He took a sheet from his mattress and tied one end to a cup hook and the other to drawer knob on a bureau beside his portmanteau so as to afford her a greater degree of privacy. She took advantage of this and proceeded to soap under her arms and midrift.

'If you give me your clothes Gaile I can hand wash them with some of my own by the waterfall. You can borrow a nightshirt and one of my great coats until yours dry out.'

Unlive returned to the waterfall with a basket including her dirty clothes. He pummelled them against the rocky bank until the soap had drained and rinsed them under the waterfall. These rags were all she had left, the sentiment was not lost on him and he told himself that he had broken so many of the rules he had set about remaining detached from situations.

When he returned he judged the wind just strong enough to dry her clothes, so he hung a line from the wagon to a nearby tree. Gaile wore his great coat, its enamel buttons and dark colour set off her hair. Unlive smiled to her as he climbed back in under the canvas.

It was now Gaile's turn to watch as he moved closer to Niamh's fragile body. He asked her if he might wrap her baby in a bandage and she agreed. Titus took a small cross he had found on the battlefield the year before and he wrapped it in the bandages with the baby. He then gave Gaile the herbal remedy mixed with a measure of Kingsevil, which settled her stomach. She placed the dead infant carefully into the empty laundry basket and they set out together. Gaile's face was partly hidden by the high collar of his great coat, his nightshirt tied around her waist with cord. This unlikely pairing reached the hole dug hours earlier by the tree. Unlive said a prayer, one that he had learnt because he had heard it many times during burials for those lost in service. He included some lines about the infant that personalized it for its mother. She was visibly lost in the new emptiness she had uncovered. Unlive took the tiny body and placed it in the ground he had dug. Gaile made the sign of the cross on her breast and almost instinctively threw a fistful of earth into the hole. He waited a moment and took the shovel and reclaimed the earth.

Thomond Babbage was philosophical about the news from Belfast. It was a 'no', but it was a 'no' that had things attached to it. This was a 'no' from a man who had refused nearly half a million pounds for a property that was decrepit, suffused with damp and bordered on all sides by an area due for redevelopment. That was intriguing all by itself, never mind the character of the man. Previously he had purchased from people only too willing to lay a claim to a site and then hike up the price. But this was different; the man had no interest in the money and that made him all the more appealing to Thomond Babbage. It conjured images in an ill man's mind of hard-bitten farmers who stashed all their money in a mattress and when that was full they kept large numbers of banknotes in their tractor seats or wrapped up in the outside cistern above the toilet. These people were the kind that held up busy traffic as they shuttled farmwives to grocery stores in archaic vehicles that barely reached thirty miles per hour on open roads. Here was a man who obviously didn't need the aspirational trappings of modern life, took what he needed and no more. A man who didn't turn his back on life but perhaps had seen so much of it that he knew its fickle secrets.

Yes, the more Thomond dwelled on the owner in Belfast, armed with the reams of information gathered by Richelieu-Mazarin, the more he wanted to meet this person. Would his doctor let him travel though? Would his family kick up a fuss? Would it make any difference in the end? He thought he knew some answers, but this was his cause and if it brought about his end, then at least he died trying. He had built this idea up in his mind to such a degree that he believed by going over there himself he could get some relief from the pain. He decided to wrap the whole idea up as a holiday to the 'Old Country'. He could tell the boys whatever they wanted to hear about his wanting to trace old roots and distant relations. Thomond would bring his doctor of course, he could afford to and the itinerary would revolve around his need for a clean room wherever he went, but it was possible. He knew one thing for certain time was running out for him, a rich man without a cure who had stopped panicking long ago. His doctor had been with him since the illness took hold, they were very free with each other, grumpy and reliant. His name was Archibald Wilton and he was in reality semi-retired and looked upon Thomond as more a family member than a patient. Archibald knew something was up when Thomond asked him round to watch the Red Sox game. He sat there nursing a Jack Daniels and Coke until the bottom of the ninth.

'Thomond, how long have we known each other?' he asked.

'Let me see, Watergate that was 72, or 74?'

'Thomond you know darn well when Watergate was. You also know that I'm a Brooklyn Dodgers fan and you asked me round here to watch the Boston Red Sox!'

'Well I was kinda at a loose end and thought of you, you want a potato chip?'

'With bourbon? You must be kidding. I advise you not to eat too much of them today.'

'Advice taken. I knew I paid you for something!'

Thomond is allowed two ice-cold Buds per baseball match and his long term addiction to starchy crisps soak up the wind from the beer.

'You're up to something, I can smell it, you want to ask me a favour, well I won't let you borrow anything else until you return the Bob Newhart box set I lent you two years ago.'

'Two years ago?' Thomond asks.

'Yes, and I can see from here that you have now secreted it among your DVD collection in the display unit over there.'

'Two years, you have harboured this for that length of time?'

'Why certainly, the 'Driving Instructor' is my favourite sketch of all time.'

With that Thomond rises out of his lazy boy chair and walks over to the cabinet and retrieves the box set, missing a vital period of play as the baseball climaxes. He winces to himself and sets the collection down beside Archibald.

'Look what you made me do Archie, I don't know how to operate the remote to watch that again.'

'You mean you can rewind live action footage on your remote?' asks Archie.

'I did once, before I lost the instructions, the boys know how to do it, but what the heck!'

'I must get one of those things. Mrs Wilton won't know what hit her when I can have instant replay after one of her tirades about this and that.'

'Listen Archie, I will buy you an instant replay box, I promise, if you will accompany me on a trip to Ireland.'

Archie looks away from the television and down at his bourbon, then takes a gulp and forms the words in his mouth.

'Ireland, Thomond! I strongly advise against this.'

Thomond turns the volume right down, the game was only a rouse to get Archie settled. The outcome in the room was always more important.

'Archie I think my body can take the journey. You coming with me can only help, it's probably the last trip I will take.'

'I agree there. If you want to usher yourself off in a hurry, then a long haul flight just outta do it for you!'

Thomond rises to the drinks cabinet and refreshes Archie's bourbon.

'There was no easy way to ask you. Certainly not in front of the boys, but I thought if I could convince you that I was strong enough to fly.'

'You know it's not just the flight, the tiredness, the jetlag, it would be doubly punishing on your weakened constitution. As your doctor and your friend, I strongly advise against doing this.'

'So you'll come with me then?' asks Thomond.

'If you insist, but because I know that when you have made up your mind, then that's it, no going back.'

'I will arrange for you to tell the boys that the trip has your blessing.'

Thomond cracks his tin of Bud against Archie's glass as his doctor shakes his head as to what he had just conceded.

7

Will Donaghoe never dreamt about Mr Unlive again. He did remember some of last nights dream though, the bit where he tried to call to Jeff Buckley from the riverbank at Wolf Harbor along the Mississippi river. Buckley had his back to him and was holding his guitar above his head, fully clothed in the water. A tugboat obscured his view for a moment and Buckley was gone below the water, he drowned with his boots on.

The office dynamic at Lydon & Dye rotated, no Gordon so no custodian to sweat the hours, to rein in the new blood. A replacement had to be found and the choices were legion. The frontrunner was Castor Felton, a former stable mate of Will's. Castor was rarely called by his first name as he cultivated a reliance on distant formality to assuage any personal vulnerability. Castor had a singular sense of his own purpose and perpetuated his meteoric rise through the ranks by stealth and connivance. He was the consummate mind gamer, a devourer of cross words and solitary past times. Castor had morphed from Will's confident and former flat mate to the diffident marble man who jettisoned relationships that might slur or blemish his rise. Castor's appointment would usher in the rush of officiousness that Gordon, to his credit, had once absorbed with the tenacity of an ancient sequoia. Gordon had been on training courses with Castor, Gordon was discrete, but he broke a few pencils when he mentioned the contortions that Castor would get himself into to impress the bosses.

Castor's main rival for the position was Lydia Hampton. Lydia worked for a rival firm and was headhunted by young Mr Retchett, partly because she was dynamic, but mostly because young Mr Retchett couldn't take his eyes off her chest. She despised him of course and she was bi-sexual, a fact that made Toby Retchett a figure of ridicule, as everyone but him knew her orientations. Lydia was a confident power dresser; she could back this up with conversational team building skills that empowered her staff, making individuals feel valued. Lydia was the obvious choice in Will's eyes, but that remained to be seen. Gordon certainly had broken no pencils at the mention of her name. She was popular, not least because she knew how to win the favour of both sexes, by working hard and playing even harder with boys and girls. She used her attraction in a subtle way, blending her experience with the approachability of a big sister. She never bowed to office romances and kept her private life intriguingly just over the horizon. Lydia was a motivator, both she and Castor shone, but with a different intent. She was less selfish, she had got this far using her wits and glamour, he was a back climbing, sleeked individual who cultivated authority with the accuracy of a crop sprayer.

The interviews were to be held on Monday morning at the flagship office. Try as he may, Will couldn't get the day off, or even work from home, as it was customary to have a team meeting on Mondays. The line up if you could call it that included the two frontrunners and a brace of ambitious usurpers from hinterland branches. The experience would test their metal and give them confidence for the next time. Will's desk at the foot of the stairs to the client suites would be a showcase for dapper suits and power dressing as they filtered by. The thought made him cringe, but Gemma had sensed his unease hours earlier and reminded him of the things that mattered while they held each other close in bed that morning.

She confided with wisdom beyond her tender years, that few of us actually get what we want in our professional lives, those that do are forced to make sacrifices and change dramatically. She said that we lose something of ourselves if we give too much of our time chasing ambition. Will smiled at her and asked if she had actually met Mr Unlive because it was like quoting from his hymn sheet. She said that he couldn't have been all that bad if he realised that work and the pursuit of money wasn't everything. What a calming influence Gemma was for him, he had his faults, some were all too visible, but he had her love and that was his shield. If he told her, she would probably call him a dick, so he held her curves tight instead until it was time to get up.

Will tapped his steering wheel that morning in time to Jeff Buckley's 'Lover, you should've come over'. It had special significance for him after the dream the night before. He didn't even mind not being able to find his regular parking space, Gemma had worked her magic on him and he was within her force field. Sandra Morton brought him over a cup of coffee and perched on his desk beside the snow globe.

'I went to see Spandau Ballet last night at the Waterfront,' she said.

'Really, so legal wrangles and mutual antipathy aside, how did they sound?' Will asked sarcastically.

'Well it wasn't packed, but they were brilliant. Tony could lose a few pounds, the guy on sax still has the quiff and the Kemp brothers are still fit. They did all the hits and I loved it.'

'Tony, don't get me started, his voice always reminded me of a fog horn warning ships of hazardous reefs.'

'That's not very nice Will, he still has it.'

'Well, I suppose he got tired of parading himself on the c-list circuit of can't cook so don't bother and I'm in a ball gown get me out of here.'

Just as Sandra crossed her arms in a fake huff at his last remark, Castor Felton approached his desk.

'Will Donaghoe as I live and breathe.'

'Sandra Morton, this is Castor Felton.'

Sandra shakes his hand and instinctively knows that Felton is a cold individual, she makes her excuses and returns to her desk.

'Castor, here for an interview? They are running a little late this morning from what I can make out.'

'Fine, I expected as much, thought I would chew the fat with you.

Were you not tempted to apply?'

'Not really my sort of thing, maybe a few years ago, but not now.'

'Well the interview experience might have done you good, sharpened your game.' Castor replies.

This is verbal tennis and Will was prepared for it this morning, he hates Castor and everything he stands for, but the knack of not letting it seep out is prerequisite.

'I have gone as far as I want to go with this company Castor. Gordon is a good manager, old school, he ran this place smoothly.'

'Gordon is a laughing stock, he's finished and he knows it. This place needs authority and leadership, a change of direction.'

Will is almost tempted to rise and give a victory salute, but catches himself on and soaks up the diatribe in a way Gemma would have been proud.

'Good luck with that Castor.' Not one ounce of sincerity in his voice. Castor turns and reaches for the handrail that leads up to the client interview suites, looking around the office as he does so. Will shakes his head, ridding him of the memories of that man and begins to answer an email from Jodi regarding the impending visit of a pair of Americans who are anxious to meet with the owner of the Joy's Entry property.

1798

An era, like a calendar year all too soon becomes outdated and cast aside as an unfashionable memory. The life spans of recollections about great storms, bad harvests, droughts and diseases become frayed and blurred with the telling over time. Presently those who kept attentions with their tales by open fires on velvet evenings would themselves become statistics with their own passing. 'Late of this Parish' was a term inscribed to record the lives, some all too brief of those who struggled to make ends meet in the long eighteenth century in Ireland. If the past was indeed another country, then by consuming the Kingsevil oil, Titus Unlive had become part of the fabric of that country which now had nothing but the future to look forward to. Historians like using labels, they round things off neatly. They can reach from the attic of time and interpret their own spin on subjects such as the Stuarts or the age of reason, the age of enlightenment, or the famine. It's convenience food for the mind, neatly packaged in the certainty that a protagonist that cannot dispute because they are long since dead. Titus wasn't dead and never would be; he had outlived the census takers, the statisticians and the scribes who wrote the observations with each burial and internment. He outgrew eras with the tenacity of a fashion conscious teen, casting off a reign or regime with scant regard for its outcome. The rub here was that he couldn't interfere or be seen to interfere with fate or history for that matter. History however had a mind of it's own and no one, not even Titus Unlive could avoid it's progress across Ireland.

France was the country of his birth, France under Louis XIV was the force on mainland Europe. It was a magnet for ideologies, many of which the King flirted with and managed to keep in check during in his long tenure. One of Louis's whims was to antagonise his Protestant neighbours by evicting all the Huguenots from his country. He had enough absolute power to carry this through and of course Titus's family were victims.

How much pleasure did Titus invoke over time from the decline of the French royal house, the rise of new thinking about liberty, equality and the distribution of wealth? He consumed the writing of the period, the lofty ideals of the great French thinkers. His homeland was in meltdown and was to undergo a terror never seen since the sack of ancient Rome. He at first thought this to be cathartic; the blood when it began to pour came from the necks of the aristocrats, the ancient regime which he despised. But the outpouring didn't stop there and the terror that emerged brought down it's own protagonists and appeared to be consuming itself, opening wounds and rivalries that would take years to heal.

None of this was lost on Ireland. It was here, the first and last colony of a disingenuous neighbour where the seeds of rebellion never strayed far from the path of an uprising. Irish intellectuals along with the enlightened thinkers of Europe had been swayed by the popular revolt in France.

Revolution impaled the thoughts of the establishment, who wished nothing more than the continued suppression of the populace of whom they considered to be their chattels, worth little more thought than livestock. The methods being used in France were described in detail by the Belfast Newsletter in 1798 to those who were lucky enough to be able to read. Many saw through the violence to the end result, religious toleration, freedom, universal suffrage, equal rights for all and utmost above all, independence. Unlive read the mood and was unavoidably carried along by the ground swell of opinion. After all he was a member of a minority who were prejudiced against by the establishment, tolerated and given no rights to vote. America had thrown down the gauntlet of freedom some years earlier, now the people of his own country had risen, so why not Ireland, where injustice had been born.

The question of finance had long since loomed large. The lifetime of his pension had naturally expired, even though his actual death had never been documented. He thought it wise not to try and claim something that might lead to any speculation as to his real age. He had been frugal with his savings of course and he had fallen back on his skills as an apothecary to help keep penury at bay. He needed accommodation to rent and to trade from. He gravitated to the Huguenot enclave within the town of Belfast. It was here that he felt most comfortable, among like-minded people who had honed their skills in France and had established a burgeoning linen trade within the town. He rented rooms from a Mr Andre Bulmer at number 13 Joys Entry. The Bulmer family were respected within the Huguenot community and they owned a swathe of workshops adjacent to Ann Street in the centre of the town. The ground floor had a shop front, to which Unlive proudly hung a sign with a cobalt medicine bottle in the style of his late father's premises in London. The upstairs included living accommodation for himself and attic space which he intended to sub let to linen workers. Most importantly the property had a cellar, which afforded him enough room to store the barrels of Kingsevil oil. Titus Unlive was now part of an émigré community which was insulated but instilled a work ethic that was respected by the majority of the town. This grouping had its own place of worship, which through parsimonious endeavour became the fulcrum of the local area, being modified and extended over a period of years. The linen trade was the future for Belfast's prosperity and the Huguenots where at its heart.

Titus thought it only prudent to employ an assistant to act as a buffer in the front of shop. He was wary of the natural inclinations of gossip and intrigue that percolated within small groupings, especially where people in need of a cure are funnelled in an enclosed space. The nature and remedy of any cure is always a subject of conversation. The vendor of the cure could cultivate an air of productive aloofness and spend much of his time in a workspace that became his withdrawing room. The creation of this distance between himself and the neighbouring customers cultivated respect and made his presence more unobtrusive. He therefore came to an arrangement with Mr Bulmer for a rent discount, Titus would employ Mr Bulmer's youngest son Peter as his apprentice. Peter was 17, well known and could deflect attentions with a charm that belied his age. Peter was no academic, much as Unlive had been with his father, Titus let him work on his studies at the counter when the shop wasn't busy. Peter was popular and good looking, he knew it of course, but he wasn't big headed and treated any interest with a genuine ease. The female customers would often forget what it actually was that ailed them and leave with purchases they never intended. Peter brought exuberance that lifted the atmosphere in a dimly lit premises where damp fought with sunlight. Peter also brought his girlfriend Caroline to the workroom for intimacy on the rare occasions Mr Unlive would go out on business. Titus was aware of this of course but chose not to bring up the subject as Peter reminded him too much of himself at that age. Peter was impressionable, outgoing and an idealist, honest traits that were also malleable in the hands of others. Titus knew idealism was related to aspiration, which combined with fervour formed the basic ingredients needed to sway opinions. Peter along with others was being consumed by a romantic notion of nationhood, spurred on by great orators and the many illegal pamphlets adorning the walls that enclosed the town. Peter would often sound out Titus when the shop was empty for his opinions on the United Irishmen who sought religious tolerance in a free and independent Ireland.

'My boy, don't get caught up in this, I have seen some lost causes in my time and this has all the hallmarks of one.' he said.

'But Sir, if we all sat back and watched, then surely nothing would ever change. You have read their proclamations on freedom of beliefs and toleration for all. They want equality and an equal distribution of wealth. These are fundamental rights that belong to the few, not the majority.'

Titus closed the shutters in the shop front windows and paused before saying, 'Wealth and power have always been in the hands of the few, they control the purse strings which assuage the military and help to keep the population at bay. The Republicans are merit worthy, but they lack the support of the overwhelming majority. They appear to be united, but within their ranks they bicker over petty things, such as orders of service which splits the Catholics from the Presbyterians. They look too much to France for direction and support. The people who were planted here in the proceeding centuries, of which they form a majority in the north, look to England for support and not France.'

'You have been following this too Mr Unlive, how else would you know so much about this?'

'I know enough to stay out of it, nothing I can do can alter it's outcome. There will be a reckoning, the few in control have too much to lose, it boils down to ownership after all, deeds of entitlement in Ireland have changed hands many times. The few in control can draw on the militia, the yeomanry and arms from England to prevail. Those deluded insurgents don't know what lies in wait behind the next hedgerow because they don't have the overwhelming support of the people. The people have been divided in a way that suits the few who are in control. Divide and conquer, it's as simple as that. The Republicans are regionally disproportionate, they are spread too thin, they have leadership, but lack metal in their chain of command. They are bereft of arms in many cases and will face red-coated soldiers out in the open organised in columns with cannon. Those poor romantics will certainly put up a fight, but ultimately they will die in the fields holding pikes and farm rakes.'

'It's as if you have already seen the aftermath Mr Unlive.'

Titus didn't answer, he didn't need to, he had seen the outpouring of vengeance after revolts many times before. No quarter was given to those seen as traitors by the establishment. Peter's ardour for the cause was no less diminished by the misgivings of a back street quack.

Later that summer the young man would have his answer. Belfast was placed under martial law with a curfew by its militia commander General Nugent. No one was able to leave the town limits after nightfall, rumour was ripe within and troops of yeomanry were dispersed from

Belfast and Lisburn to Antrim town for a fateful confrontation. Unlive had predicted the outpouring, the valiant failure of farmhands and lay preachers against ranks of organised infantry. The rebel support was fickle at best and many had simply melted into the night without ever seeing the enemy that awaited them. They had no cannon and precious little cavalry to support the brave exultations by men like Henry Joy McCracken. The outcome was never in doubt and the rebels were soon dispersed to the hills and hunted relentlessly by the mounted yeomanry. It never ceased to amaze Titus when he heard of the zeal used in pursuit of the hunted, as if it was reduced to the level of a foxhunt and the quarry ceased to be a person anymore if they dared to wear a green ribbon. Bad luck was a charm attached to this ribbon and McCracken was soon recognised and taken into custody, swiftly tried and sentenced. The mounted yeomanry made great play at his efforts to address the crowd in the Cornmarket before his hanging and drowned out many of his final words. Titus had opted to stay at home that day even though the throng was yards from his door. The afternoon was given over to the mob, many of whom were bribed to enthuse and charge the hostile atmosphere. Peter was there of course, Caroline was with him in the scrum around the hastily erected gallows. Peter managed to perch her onto a wooden scaffold out of harms way and they saw the dignity McCracken bore right up to the end. Caroline looked away as his body struggled in the void at the end of the rope, then it just swayed slowly to a standstill. She wept for a man she didn't know, who's honesty struck her and many others in the crowd and a great moan was heard as the authorities cut him down swiftly enough as part of an arrangement with McCracken's sister. She could have the body if he was interred before nightfall. Peter watched as they cut the limp shape down, the red and purple hews of scarring around the neck were visible in contrast to the clean shirt he wore. His family were allowed access and gathered his crumpled form as the crowd parted in deference, some reaching to touch the body for as if it were a relic. As they did so, Peter was nudged from behind by a man he didn't recognise. The man said nothing and fixed his eyes on Peter as he placed a note in the boy's hand along with three silver coins. He was gone before Peter could form any words.

'Who was that?' Caroline asked.

'I have no idea.'

'What does the note say?'

'Urgent. For Mr Unlive.'

Peter helped Caroline down from the scaffold and they made their way against the flow back down Joys Entry. Titus was at the window with a cup and saucer in his hands.

'A grim business my boy and no mistake.' he said as they entered.

'Sir I was given this note not five minutes ago, it is marked urgent for your attention.'

Titus took it from Peter, tore it open and held it up to the light. Then without saying anything he grabbed his cape and leather satchel and went into his workroom. He emerged shortly afterwards, the satchel was heavier than before, he locked the workroom door and told Peter to keep an eye on things as he had to go out for a while. Peter thought it best not to ask what the letter had said and was also thankful that he and Caroline would have some time alone together in the shop. Caroline was visibly upset from the hanging and he could comfort her away from the glare of the throng outside.

Titus covered the distance as best he could, it wasn't far, but it was fraught with ribald peasantry, off duty soldiers cavorting, shouting and making the route hazardous. It was less than half a mile to the McCracken's house in Rosemary Lane, but with the food stalls and drunken masses parading through the entries, it seemed to take ages. Souvenir sellers plied their wares, the morbid toys with mechanical gallows complete with miniature trap doors and tiny coffins carved in every detail. The whores in their unkempt wantonness, open legged, leaning against alley walls offering relief in every form to those who would risk infection. He waved off their advances, keeping his leather satchel firmly under his cape and before long he was filtered out at a courtyard in Rosemary Lane. A crowd had also formed here too, but it had a different, reverential flavour. Titus was recognised by men in sombre attire and ushered in past the weeping maid and family friends. The body was laid out on the only table long enough to take it's length in the front room. Shutters were drawn and candle sconces lit, its modest proportions swelled by the number of chairs occupied by family members. A physician Titus knew had finished his examination, he folded McCracken's arms across his white shirt, raising his collar to hide the rope marks. Mary Ann, his sister approached Titus.

'You got my note Mr Unlive, thank you for coming.'

'I did Miss McCracken, I'm sorry to be here under these circumstances.'

'You are welcome in my house, thank you for being so prompt.'

'Your family are dear to all those who live in this area and beyond.' She took Unlive's hand and led him over to the table and the body of her brother.

'I know his neck is broken Mr Unlive, but his body is still warm, is there nothing you can do to help revive him?'

The poor woman he thought, reduced to this, the calm fortitude, which had carried her through the day had now been replaced by desperation at the prospect of life without her beloved brother. He was here now with an audience looking on, so he took off his cape and gave it to Mary Ann. He wouldn't need to open the leather satchel and apply any oil, what was the use in giving false hopes, he reached over the body and touched the young man's forehead. He was indeed still marginally warm to the touch, his complexion was not clammy and bore the aspect of sleeper.

The physician was still in the room and shook his head as Titus caught his eye. Unlive rolled back Henry's sleeve and pressed his wrist around the man's elbow. He thought he had captured the faintest of pulses, but he couldn't be sure, so he opened the young man's mouth with one hand and held a mirror over the mouth with his other. The young rebel leader was dead. The oil would not revive him now, he was gone from this world, Titus reached out for Mary Ann and said,

'Come now, we need a winding sheet to wrap the body, I believe you have been given permission to bury him before nightfall?'

Mary Ann had her answer in the finality of his words; it was time to ignite the readiness that employs the grief stricken. Her family prepared Henry's corpse and a plain coffin was brought into the room and presently two men lifted his body into it.

Torches were lit along the route to St. George's church, the rabble and the rowdy were corralled by the sympathetic and the procession was dignified with many joining its length before reaching the graveyard steps. Titus didn't go to the interment, instead he cut back through the entries and surprised Peter and Caroline at play in the workroom.

'Sweet Jesus.' Peter cried.

'I think I did you a favour there my boy, and you too Caroline. I know that you can't keep your hands off each other, but for god's sake be a bit more careful.'

'Forgive me Sir, I guess with we got caught up in the events of the day.'

Peter was right, something had to be done to release the torpid nature of that day. The perverse justice meted out as entertainment for the masses had assuaged some hungers, many found alcohol to be the perfect companion while others sought physical comfort as a way of proving their lives to be emphatic. For who did not want to feel alive in the midst of all this death? Titus of course had seen it all before, he imagined himself clinging to a chimney pot on his rented rooftop looking out over Belfast. The entries were arterial from up here, people scampered in the flow, sometimes they huddled in corners to form clots outside coffee houses. Fires would be set and emit smoke to announce supper for the wealthier classes in the better off districts with neatly aligned roof shingles. The town was belted in by a red-coated curfew, the price in blood for the loss of a days trading was costly indeed.

Titus could make out the caves in the distant hill where the rebels had once sheltered, a blackened hollow outline which had swallowed up their dreams for generations to come. No embrocation that was within his remit to concoct would ease the scars of this patient.

Archie was right to voice his concerns over Thomond flying. The journey had taken its toll on a man now old before his time. The necessary precautions were implemented, but still Thomond was exhausted by the time they had reached their hotel in Belfast. Archie had stipulated that they share adjoining rooms and the hotel complied, they had two executive suites on the top floor with only the pool and sauna/fitness area as company. Archie commandeered part of the fitness area as a clean room to facilitate Thomond. Richelieu-Mazarin had contacted Lydon & Dye to arrange a meeting with Will Donaghoe and get some more background on Mr Unlive. Thomond was still sleeping at three pm when Will rang his suite.

'Hello is that Doctor Wilton?'

'Yes who is calling?'

'My name is Will Donaghoe from Lydon & Dye property consultants. Did you both have a pleasant trip?'

'Mr Donaghoe, that man shouldn't have left Boston, but I know how pig headed he can be, so I accompanied him. It has caught up with him now and I have given him a sedative to help him rest. I think he will be up for visitors in another day or so. Can I ring your office when he is feeling stronger?

'Of course, if there is anything else I can help you with just let me know.'

Thomond heard the call being directed to the other room, he was not out for the count just yet, a strange bed in a new town had kept him alert. The doubts came flooding in as he turned in the bedclothes to distract himself from them. He thought about his late wife, what would she think of the hare brained idea, travelling half way around the globe looking for some miracle cure. Did he not gain comfort from the fact that he would soon be with her anyway in the next life? He looked for any grains of consolation, but as he did, he realised that he had compromised others in this pursuit, not just himself. Archie would follow him anywhere, but this was different. He imagined windmills beyond the bedclothes and fixed his head along the pillow in line with them until finally he fell asleep. Archie peered in around the door and saw that the sedative had done its work. He thought he might explore the hotel further and so he grabbed his jacket and went down to the lobby. As much as he had harangued Thomond, Archie was enjoying sitting watching the great and the good of Belfast filter in and out of the former banker's floor space, while he nursed a well earnt Jack Daniels and cola. The drink waxed his thoughts, he took in the ornate setting, the ambient décor and the snobs it attracted. A waiter brought him a copy of a late edition local paper and he mused at what passed for news around here. He acclimatised and allowed himself another drink before taking the elevator back to the top floor to check on his friend.

As much as it pained him to do so, Will had to contact Mr Unlive again. His phone was on answer machine when he called so he decided to do it in person. He would have to clear it with his new office manager Lydia Hampton. Lydia had trounced Castor to the role, much to Will's glee.

She was making her mark on the office already, breaking down cliques with her managerial charms. Lydia was the opposite of Gordon, which wasn't a bad thing, both were smart but approached the net differently. Gordon gave you more chances and even took the wrap if things fell through, Lydia gave you one chance to shine and wrote you off if you didn't. She had rationalised roles already and made things more competitive for the hitters, which kept them anxious to please. This was the new way, her way, her rules, served up in a style that oozed confidence. She micro managed people, latching on to an idea and delivering her own spin naturally so as not to take all the credit. Will liked her and from what he could tell she liked him.

'Lydia can I have a word?'

Her door was always open, another new policy.

'Have those figures for me first thing Dermot.' She waved Will in. 'The developer gave us first refusal on this and we can match their percentages okay? Thanks.'

She turned authoritatively to Will as she replaced the handset.

'Will, how's it going?'

'Fine, I was wondering if you wouldn't mind if I called on a client after lunch today. It would mean missing your team meeting.'

'I'm sure we will manage, who is the client?'

'Mr Unlive at Joys Entry.'

She clicks his details on her Mac.

'He isn't selling Will. Do you hope to change his mind?'

'Well no actually, the buyer has come over from America and wants to meet with him and as I have a relationship, so to speak.'

'I see, it must be important for them to come all this way.'

'Yes it does seem excessive, American bravado probably.'

'Very well then, take as much time as you need to set this one up okay.'

'Thanks Lydia.'

'If you pull this one off Will, I won't have to let out your chair.'

He smiled at her instinctively, she more than half meant it and he knew it. Lydia was here to cut out the dead wood, she was taking mental notes about the staff all the time and Will wasn't exempt. Who could blame her he thought, his targets had been reached, but that didn't take away from the fact that he was peripheral to the robbery and the fall out that it had on the image of the firm. Will had lunch with Sandra Morton, he treated her this time at Café Anjou. It was subdued today, they found it easy to get seated and she ordered the usual corn cob soup while he stuck loyally to his panini wrap. Orton's ghost hovered around their dalliance and soon Will asked her had she heard from him.

'He's taken this badly, poor thing.' she said.

'He's lost a friend as well as his job I suppose.' said Will.

'I spoke to him last week and he was thinking of finding Sally. I told him that was pointless, if the Police couldn't find him/her what chance had he?' she asked.

'I know, he needs to focus on himself and what he is going to do. Orton is made of stronger stuff, I'm certain he will come through this okay. He will have trust issues and will have to stop shooting his mouth off with idle gossip. So maybe he will have learnt something about himself.'

'He kind of did like being the focus of so much attention, but that was superseded by Sally,' she said.

Will knew his role over lunch was to listen to Sandra. Everyone in the office was insecure about the future, not least her. Change at the top brought on by a robbery had repercussions that sharpened everyone's game. He walked her back from the café and tried to reassure her, maybe they had stuck their heads in the ground for too long and this was the wake up call in the form of Lydia. At the office door he hugged Sandra and she perked up as he went on down the street trying to remember where he had parked his car. He turned up 'Family Snapshot' by Peter Gabriel as it came on Nostalgia FM.

Mr Unlive was in and was more than a little surprised to see Will at his door. He never did work out how to rewind his answer machine and consequently didn't hear Will's numerous messages.

'Mr Donaghoe please come in, I feel that we left on bad terms.' he said.

'Thank you for seeing me. If I'm honest I didn't expect to be back here again myself.'

'Then we can sort out any bad feelings, I never meant to create an atmosphere between us.'

'I wanted to let you know that my American clients are here in Belfast and they are anxious to meet with you.'

Titus bolted the door behind them in the hallway.

'Will, no amount of money could persuade me to leave this place, you know that by now.'

'I do Sir, I think they just want to talk with you, would you consider meeting them?'

'These people know about the oil Mr Donaghoe, I know you didn't tell them, they knew about its existence long before you did. They have left a trail all over this island, places where I have treated people with the oil. I have always managed to stay one step ahead until now. They have been buying up rumours and purchasing land, digging in the clay for traces of any casks.'

'All I know is that a man and his doctor have travelled thousands of miles in the hope of talking with you.'

'So one of them is ill. Illness can lead to desperation, it can also lead to great clarity of thought. I wonder what his intentions are? If they were malicious then surely they would have broken into my house by now as Ryan did.'

'I really don't think they are the type Mr Unlive. Ryan was desperate. He was addicted to the oil, no more, no less. He wanted it for himself, he had no intention of sharing it with the Americans.'

'Perhaps you are right. I sometimes think I am cursed with this ability to out grow an age. In the length of time I take to trust someone, they have used up their own lifetime. Do you know how hard it is not to be able to form real relationships with people? To be able gain their trust and friendship. Most importantly, to not be able to satisfy a woman?' Will squirms a little at the prospect.

'I have tried to live among generations of people. You see yourself getting older Mr Donaghoe, it plays on your mind. Imagine all the people of your age on this island, not just those who you know and are acquainted with. Pack these people onto a passenger liner in Belfast Lough. Every cabin and berth is full to capacity with people of your age, the promenade areas and even the lifeboats are consumed with those of your generation. Now if you will, imagine that liner leaving Belfast once a day for the next fifteen days. That is the number of generations I have lived amongst.'

'When you put it like that Sir, I can see why you would be so wary of any attachment.'

'What is the good in attachment, if they can't share their life with you? How would I ever explain to anyone that I will still be exactly the same when they are frail? Even the most rational minds would have difficulty understanding it.'

'I understand it Sir. It took some taking in, and I still haven't quite got round to explaining it to my girlfriend, but I do understand.'

'Will, I came to you first in your dreams, I left you able to dismiss them, whilst I also got you familiar with the idea that I was immortal. How many times were you left shaking your head at the very thought on your awakening? I could never try and explain myself to every person who came in close contact with me. I would have ended up in Bedlam long since if I did. I get to witness the rise and demise of those who would leave their mark on the land. I can't alter anything, but I can help those who deserve it. I have kept the oil from the attentions of those who would wish to exploit it, thus far.'

'I really don't think these Americans want to exploit you for the oil Sir.'

'That remains to be seen, however I will meet with them. You have my answer Mr Donaghoe.'

Will decided to make his way to the Excelsior Hotel where the Americans where staying. Central Belfast is still the hive of alleyways that Mr Unlive knew so well in the past. The hotel is not far from Joys Entry and Will entered the lobby through the swing doors. He announced himself at reception and they paged Mr Babbage's room for him. Will took a seat in one of the all-embracing leather chairs in the lobby and waited. He took in the gilded opulence, the hand painted ceiling, the stuccoed putto and shakes his head when he remembers this was once a bank.

'Mr Donaghoe?'

'Yes.'

'I'm Doctor Wilton, Mr Babbage's physician.'

'Pleased to meet you Sir.'

'Mr Babbage is still not up to seeing anyone today I'm afraid.'

'Oh really, I'm sorry to hear that. I wonder if you could pass on the message that my client has consented to your meeting with him.'

'That is good news Mr Donaghoe, I believe that will strengthen him as he has had some pretty bad days since his arrival here in Ireland.'

'Do you think he would be up to paying a house call on Mr Unlive?' asks Will.

'Certainly not until his condition stabilises somewhat. Thomond is a tough cookie, but he needs complete rest and the upheaval to get him this far has taken its toll on his health.'

'I wonder if Mr Unlive might pay him a visit here then?'

'It might be no bad thing to arrange that in a few days Mr Donaghoe, I will take a note of your cell phone number and call you when I think

Thomond is up to taking visitors. Is that okay with you?'

'Absolutely, let me know.'

Will was impressed by Dr Wilton's concern. Babbage was his patient, but he was also his best friend who's health had not rallied since they had checked in to the hotel just over five days before. Constant supervision and intensive care couldn't stop Thomonds rapid deterioration. Dr Wilton had adapted Thomond's suite even further and installed a large cot for himself to sleep near his friend.

'There you go again Archie, fussing and fretting.' Thomond said dryly from under his oxygen mask.

'This clean tent is not good enough. You will just have to make use of the mask when you struggle with your breathing.'

'That would be all the time then except meal times, when you feed me that crap. I haven't been out of this room since I got to Ireland, we might as well be in Baltimore!'

'I don't think I have seen a hotel like this in Baltimore. For your information, you had a visitor today. Mr Donaghoe from the realtor's came over earlier. He met with that Mr Unlive character you are so interested in.'

'Really? What did he have to say?'

'The guy wants to meet with you. I said that he had better come over here as you weren't well enough to pay house calls.'

'Thank you Archie.'

Dr Wilton could see the optimism rise in his friends face for a moment. The juxtaposition of gilded bed and heart rate monitors enclosed in plastic sheeting couldn't be more severe and made for a movie set rather than a boutique hotel. He took out his diary and rang Will Donaghoe. 'Will, I know you have only just left the lobby, but would you consider getting Mr Unlive to pay us a visit sooner rather than later?'

'I will contact him straight away Sir.'

Will was in Victoria's Secret when Dr Wilton rang. Something in what

Mr Unlive had said about relationships had crystallized in his mind. He was picking out lingerie for Gemma with a very helpful assistant who was a similar size to his girlfriend. Her name was Sarah and she was used to gauche males who were shy about purchasing such items. Sarah knew this was an impulse buy and that Will had just darted in, but he was trying and that was the main thing. She picked out some lingerie which she couldn't resist and held them up on her figure to give him an impression. He could see Gemma loving this and he pictured her laughing at him sizing up another woman. He took the first set he was shown and at the cash desk he asked Sarah where she had got her snub toe heels. She told him that they were part of the new Dita collection available on the third floor. He took the escalator and hunted out a pair of size three snub toes for Gemma. He was more than a little pleased with himself, he felt like he was a truant with a stolen wallet. Will took the stairs down to the basement of the mall, which had enclosed everything in its proximity but Titus Unlive's house. He sat in his car in the darkness for a moment, the packages on the back seat.

Was this the level Ryan had surveyed? Did he even go deeper than this? Where these concrete pillars built over the tunnels that led out in all directions? They must be close. He took out his mobile phone and rang Mr Unlive.

'Sir, I'm sorry to bother you again so quickly today. I was wondering when would suit you to pay a visit to the Americans?'

'Well I don't know, I expected you to bring them here.'

'Mr Babbage is too weak to move Sir, could we both pay him a visit?'

'I don't see why not, although this is somewhat irregular, when were you thinking of Mr Donaghoe?'

'The man is ill Sir, very weak from what I gather. Would it be out of the question to visit him now?'

'Are you nearby Will?'

'Yes Sir I am.'

'Well then we have no time to lose. Meet me at my house as soon as you can.' said Titus.

The two men walked in silence to the Excelsior hotel. It was late afternoon and those lucky enough were heading home to avoid the daily logjam that settles around the City Hall. Titus carried a Gladstone bag and Will couldn't help but think how typical of the man it was. Mr Unlive he thought, he made do and mended, he had stared out eons with the patience of a croupier. The contents of the bag, he knew to be among other things, the Kingsevil oil. This survivor was going to treat a man he had never met before with the miracle oil that had brought so much hope to many over the intervening centuries. Will saw the quiet determination of the man beside him, no questions need be asked. Babbage was another person in need and Unlive would treat him no differently than the rest. Dr Wilton was waiting in the lobby for them. 'My name is Titus Unlive, are you the physician?'

'I am Mr Unlive, my name is Dr Archibald Wilton. Thank you for coming here at such short notice. Really, I don't know what else to say.'

'Before we go up I need to know what medication he is on and his full case background.'

'I expected as much and I have a file here for you to inspect Mr Babbage's condition.'

Titus took the file and headed for an unoccupied annexe with plush seats to the right of the main reception area. His weathered shoes were just visible to Will and Dr Wilton as he settled down to read the case history. Will gestured to the Doctor to follow him into the bar area.

'I have two private nurses providing care twenty four seven. This is the worst I have seen him for years Mr Donaghoe.'

Will could see emotion in his tired and pallid face and asked Archibald if he wanted anything from the bar.

'I'm partial to a Jack Daniels and cola mostly, the nurse can beep my pager if she needs me, but I don't see why I couldn't have a drink with you. Thank you.'

'Gentlemen that drink will have to wait.' Titus gave the file back to Doctor Wilton and they knew it was time to take the lift to the top floor. On the way up Will noticed that Dr Wilton seemed to size up Mr Unlive, this was the man Thomond had made so much fuss about. In this context he supposed that Titus did look quite diminutive when everything else was considered. Will had reconciled the fact that Titus was over 300 years old, but even when he heard himself say it he instinctively shook his head. As he did so he glanced over and for a moment caught the knowing look on Unlive's face. The man had read his mind again, the confusion mixed with honesty, the desire and the trepidation that spewed from the thought patterns in his head. What a dissembling mix for anyone to try and read never mind deal with. Dr Wilton led them through a suite of rooms and into Thomond's bedroom. Thomond waved Dr Wilton over.

'That nurse is trying to kill me Archie, I swear she gave me a bed bath today that put my back out of joint for good this time.'

'I'm sure she knows what she is doing Thomond, you are just a bit cranky what with the medication and being bed ridden.'

Thomond looked over Archie's back and saw the two figures waiting patiently.

'Please come nearer gentlemen, grab a chair each of you,' he beckoned.

Titus proceeded with a chair and placed it at the head of the bed in line with Thomond. Before sitting down he shook Thomond firmly by the hand. Thomond's grip had lost none of it's strength and he wanted to show Titus his appreciation.

'Thank you for coming Mr Unlive. You have made a long journey worthwhile.'

'You have spent a lot of time and energy coming to see me, it was only fair that I come this short distance to visit with you.' said Titus.

'You are what kept me going, believing in you, that you actually existed. That got me this far, the belief that you would help me.'

'I know now that I was wrong about you,' Titus interjected. 'I was wrong to pay heed to the gossip about the intentions of a pharmaceutical company. It was rumour that fed my speculation that you wanted to use my oil for your company.'

Thomond looked genuinely shocked at Mr Unlive's revelation. He realised that his actions in Ireland might have been misconstrued by anyone not privy to his condition.

'My god of course! You must have felt cornered. I was purchasing land that you had frequented. I didn't think of it that way until now. You thought I wanted to obtain this oil you mentioned for personal gain.'

'I have been alone for too long I think Mr Babbage. I won't go into it, but seclusion does stimulate the imagination and only by mixing with people such as yourself can I rid myself of any negativity. Babbage, now that is an interesting name, not local, but of Irish origins, am I right?'

'You are most definitely right Sir! My first name is Thomond, a name that has been handed down through my family since the time of the famine.' Thomond settled back on copious pillows.

'Babbage, for some reason the name reminds me of Limerick. Would I be on the right track?' asked Titus.

'You are Mr Unlive. They came from Limerick originally.' Thomond's face lit up as his pain subsided momentarily with the recollection.

1845

'The old keep in the bridge over the Shannon water. In the autumn of 1845 I came across a family of seven, two parents and five children. I remember them clearly. I had led my horse to the flooded embankment to drink when I saw a boy vainly fishing in the torrent. I told him that the swell was too strong to fish in after all the heavy rain that had fallen previously. The boy said he was desperate to catch something as his family had not eaten properly for days and his sister was growing too weak to leave the keep. Instinctively I asked to meet his family and I let him hold my stirrup as he led me back up the path to the bridge. His father had been watching us from the turret but hadn't intervened I think because he saw that I was genuinely concerned. The boy pushed open a lead studded door which was at the entrance of the keep. We entered into a large ground floor room that had recently been used to shelter cattle at one end judging by the smell. The end we occupied had been sectioned off and bore all the hallmarks of a grain store, the residue of which littered the floor. The poor devils had been reduced to milling this residue into a pulp, which they had eaten mixed with river water until the mix ran out three days previously. The boy's father came out of the shadows and approached me. I think he said his name was Finbar Babbage, I could see he was a proud man who had fallen on hard times. He put both hands on the boys shoulders and apologised for his son's actions. I said there was no need and I asked if I might see the girl who was poorly. The father motioned to say that he couldn't pay for my services, whereupon I reassured him not to concern himself. His wife led me up the stone steps with no handrail to the first floor and within I saw that the floor had been recently swept and at the far end under a glassless window lay a figure on a straw cot. This wretched figure tried to sit up as I approached, only to slump back on the straw. I knelt beside the girl and stroked her head, it was burning up. I told the mother to wait with her while I went back to my wagon. I asked the boy to accompany me, for the life of me I cannot remember his name. I gave him a sack full of maize and told him to return with it to his father. I then poured a measure of Kingsevil oil from the cask. I grabbed a patterned throw and a large wooden bowl and made my way back to the keep. I told Finbar that this was a cereal wheat which he could use as a staple for his family until they were able to find better sustenance. I mixed some of the maize into the wooden bowl, adding water and finally poured in the measure of oil. I brought it upstairs to the girl who lay there. I am sure I asked her mother what the girl's name was, but I'm afraid I can no longer remember it either. I fed the girl sparingly and then handed the bowl to her mother and told her to do the same. I called for her father and told him that they needed to board up the window and prepare a fire to be lit in the room where the girl lay. She had a fever and was oblivious to temperature changes as her body fluctuated from cold to hot. She would need to sweat out this fever and that might take a number of days. The fitter boys were employed gathering kindling and firewood, the large chimney space on the first floor of the keep was cleared of debris and a fire was set within. I could see that a sense of purpose had returned to their ranks and with that hope bore fruit in their hearts again. I decided to wait with them. I shared my store of salt beef and maize amongst them and they trusted me implicitly. At meal times, I rationed out a measure of the oil to each family member and they grew stronger daily as a result. The girl, whose name I forget, came through the illness and hugged me when she was strong enough. I stayed with them near the keep by the bridge over the Shannon for seven days, longer than I had ever allowed myself previously with anybody. Finbar confided that he wanted to get his family to America, where they could prosper and be beholden to no one. I said that the maize I had given them was from America, it was nutritious and could be farmed on land that stretched as far as the eye could see. He said he would want to plant such a crop on a farm there one day. His boys sat by his side as we shared hopes in the firelight while the girls dozed on the straw cot behind us.

America was what kept them going then and now you have come from there to seek me out so that I can help your family again. I am sorry that I didn't make the connection sooner, I am a suspicious old man who should trust people more.'

Thomond was in rapture. Unlive's recollection had rekindled names he had almost forgotten. Finbar Babbage did indeed take his family safely to the new world and they headed west to the arable farmland in Iowa. The boys would grow strong and were educated to believe in their abilities. From a strain of that family, Thomond was derived. He could map out his family tree in his mind later, first came the realisation that he had returned, so to speak, as a family member would do for help once more to Mr Unlive. It was as if time didn't matter to the two of them, it was unspoken and offered freely. Titus once again took Thomond's hand only this time he clasped it before reaching into his Gladstone bag.

8

Kingsevil oil is a chemical compound with the look and consistency of any domestic household cooking oil. However when applied as a balm to bare skin it transmutes into a breathable film which accelerates the healing process to any sore or wound. It can be consumed within any drink as a soothing cure and its properties meld with any liquid when measured appropriately. Titus took full advantage of its ability to numb pain when he was afflicted with a ruptured kidney stone. He had seen its healing qualities at close hand when distributing the oil to the afflicted on the many feast days at court. He had paid a price for giving himself too many measures of the oil in his delirium. The oil dissolved the stone that had once given him so much discomfort, but it had left him sterile with a mild addiction that needed quenched three times a day. Kingsevil restored his palate, giving him an appetite that couldn't over indulge, as he was prone to do previously. He washed his hair with a measure and it stopped receding noticeably the more he did so. The golden translucence gave skin a hint of youthfulness and vibrancy that replaced even Titus's wizened flesh. This was the oil used since the reign of Edward the Confessor. The medieval King's body was embalmed and cleansed using Kingsevil.

Nearly five hundred years later his tomb was disturbed in Westminster Abbey by workmen under the instructions of the Tudor usurper Henry VII. Henry wanted to make room for his own ostentatious catafalque. Their curiosity soon got the better of them and they decided to prize open the lid of Edward's tomb. They held cloths to their faces at the expected outpouring of festering decay. On removing the lid they beheld the body of a slumbering King with no outward discoloration. His skin was perfectly intact until the air in the chamber did react with the corpse causing rapid putrefaction. They shrieked at the sudden alteration and quite forgot to pillage any of the royal jewels that adorned the ermine clad corpse. Kingsevil preserved the body in life and also in death.

Titus produced a pen-like phial from his Gladstone bag, it was bound in black leather with a detachable lid.

'May I?' asked Dr Wilton.

'Be my guest.' said Titus.

Dr Wilton took the phial from its sheath and held it up to the light that was fast ebbing from the top floor hotel window. It was golden and moved like fickle mercury. Such a small amount he thought, what could this do for a man who had tried every course modern medicine could produce?

'This is the oil' he heard himself say.

With that Will rose out of his chair and joined him at the window frame. The two men turned the measure over again and again like a spirit level. Titus shrugged and looked bemused at Thomond.

'Come now, we have Mr Babbage to concern ourselves with gentlemen.'

Thomond tried to stretch under the covers, but he was weaker now than he had ever been. His usual stoicism had left him, gone with the shift change of his private nurses. One whom he liked, fancied even, the other he despised and took strength from. But now he was drained and Titus had seen that look many times before. He hadn't given up and never would, but his body had and that was maddening for a man with such a sharp business acumen. Dr Wilton handed the phial back to Titus who proceeded to pour the measure into a glass. He mixed in some still mineral water and stirred the combination with a spoon. No fizz, no reaction, the water soon regained its clear coloration. Titus bent over Thomond and removed the oxygen mask from his face.

'I want you to drink this now, and I will leave you a sufficient number of phials for you to consume another, twice daily for the next week, do you understand Mr Babbage?'

Thomond nodded and held his head back as Titus raised the glass to his mouth. He drank it down and the energy used pressed his head back into the pillows.

'Dr Wilton, I will leave these with you. Let me see, it's five fifteen now, so give him another measure at nine fifteen tonight, okay?'

Dr Wilton nodded and shook Titus by the hand. It was all he could think of and it felt the right thing to do. Will watched everything in silence, this was the oil, the reason for all the searches, the payback for all those visits, asleep or waking. He had seen it and now he believed, he saw the belief in the eyes of everyone in that room, this was bigger than all of them. This was tangible proof and now it was now coursing through Thomond's body, fighting back at the affliction that had ravaged him for so long with no end in sight. Everything Titus had told him was true and time would soon show him the results. Will escorted Titus back to Joys Entry.

'What you did back there Mr Unlive was unbelievable.'

'Whatever can you mean?' he asked.

'I can see it now, you gave that man hope.'

'He never lost hope, he never gave up, that is why I helped him.'

'I also see that you can never put a price on that. The case full of cash I offered you pales into insignificance beside what you just did for him.'

'Don't be too hard on yourself Will, it's a lot to take in and remember I have been around a lot longer than you.'

'I would never have believed it if I hadn't seen it with my own eyes.'

'Will you played your part in helping me not to cut myself off from people entirely. You taught me to trust again, I had become miserly with my emotions, disillusioned, bitter even. Time does that to people, the knocks they receive, they wear them on the inside, becoming insulated by them. I may have time on my side, but it is no friend, time has made me wise to my failings and maybe I have ironed some out as a consequence, but time has always left me invariably on my own.'

'When I realised how old you were and I accepted it to be true, I was jealous. I thought how lucky you were to outlive anybody, never get sick or frail. You put me straight about that notion. I know now how lonely you have been and frustrated too. But look what you did today for that man, what you once did for his ancestors. You are being way too hard on yourself; you have helped so many people over time, people who would have certainly died before their time. You say that you can't influence things, but you have by giving people hope. The Kingsevil would have died out, but for you, it was outmoded and unfashionable. You protected it and in the process it became part of what you are. You and the oil are now indivisible, it is the reason that you are still here today, although you sometimes pay a miserable price for that. Who would Titus Unlive have been without the oil? a footnote in history. Titus Unlive with the oil is a living part of that history.'

'Thank you Will, you certainly know how to cheer up a very old man. I had forgotten how contagious optimism could be. Around this time of day I like to take a glass of sack, would you be so kind as to join me?'

'I will Sir, with pleasure.'

Without noticing, the two men had traversed to the front door of number 13 Joys Entry, the evening sway of commuters funnelled through the passageways oblivious to their hushed conversation. Titus turned the key in the latch and it reacted with its usual reticence, the fustiness of the ages greeted them in the poorly lit hallway, familiar and yet timeless.

1941

Change maybe a stranger, but Titus was familiar with its calling card and was able to bend like a reed in the torrent to embrace the consequences.

Joys Entry where he had resided for over 250 years was one of many crooked lanes which threaded major streets together within the heart of Belfast. It was this narrow dog leg appearance which Will Donaghoe had become familiar with while pouring over the land registry discs. It was less than three storeys high in entirety, but its brooding brickwork jutted overhead as if it appeared to resent sunlight. This confinement had remained virtually unaltered in the intervening centuries. The surrounding buildings and outhouses had been modified as incomes increased or fell into disrepair as respective fortunes folded. The Bulmer family leased many properties within the entry and the rents from these leases afforded them the right to move to the more prosperous suburbs, away from the smog, the putridity of the tanneries, the rope works and the foul smelling rub of the populace. The Huguenot enclave dispersed with its own success by way of intermarrying and social climbing in many cases into the upper echelons of northern society.

Over time new arrivals took their place. Jews escaping the pogroms of eastern Europe brought with them new skills in tailoring to enhance an already long established linen trade and they also helped to oil the wheels of finance. Chinese émigrés made the long journey after the Boxer rebellion and these close knit families formed the new nucleus that thrived around Titus's home at number 13. The entry was a spring board for betterment, it was a place in transition but never transient.

The tenement blocks that made up the dog leg were workplaces at ground floor level and burgeoned with migrant families on the upper storeys. This was how Titus liked it, the reason why he stayed, these communities would move on as peer pressure, aspiration and confinement demanded. His neighbours therefore may have got to know him for a short while, but their own desire for self-improvement took them away before they realised that Titus hadn't aged a single day in all the years they might have lived beside him. He was by now a master of self-deprecation and discretion, having long since given up the role of an outmoded apothecary and had dabbled successfully as a linen merchant throughout most of the nineteenth century. He had been frugal and had made ripe investments, which enabled him to buy his property outright. Time had taught him how to live on very little, but he took care not to let himself go and was careful of his appearance. He shunned ostentation lest he draw attention to himself. He took full advantage of the Jewish tailors who sublet his upper floors, giving rent rebates to those who turned his linen into suits. He did however withdraw from the great number of rooms he owned and mothballed them as he was not one given for much entertaining. He made sufficient alterations in gas, lighting and sanitation that sufficed for the age he was currently living in. He didn't embrace new things well and that could be mistaken for eccentricity, which didn't do his image or reputation any harm within the bustle of the entry. Titus made change wait until he was ready and that was the way he liked it. Upheaval didn't bother him as he knew he would always have the time to put things right. It never occurred to him that he might need to distribute the oil on his very doorstep until the night raids came that Easter.

'Coventrate' was a term used to describe the obliteration of major towns by enemy planes during World War II. Coventry was one of the first towns outside London to receive the attentions of the Luftwaffe and was thought by many to be relatively safe being so far from the coast. It was therefore left vulnerable without sufficient anti-aircraft cover. Five hundred people lost their lives in a few hours on a moonlit evening in which the bombers were able to pick out targets at leisure. No major town was free from devastation and that included Belfast. Those children who were evacuated in preparation to rural areas, would now lie awake in strange beds listening for the drone of enemy engines. Soon enough the windowsills would start to hum and cracked putty would brake free from the panes. Crockery migrated along dresser shelves as the night bombers kept their altitude steady. Nervous livestock took shelter and fussed over themselves when the planes were directly overhead. The night formation 200 strong moved on with precision, tired navigators rubbed their eyes and unfolded yet more charts mapping out enemy terrain. Timing was everything and they didn't budget or anticipate any interceptions by the RAF and none were forthcoming. This was the optimum tactical range for a Heinkel He 111, a mid range bomber that was making a five hour round trip from a mist laden hangar along the French coast. Fuel would be running low as they reached the target area. They allowed themselves one flypast for the bomb aimers to release the incendiary flares and then would make a broad turn using Cave Hill as a guideline before sweeping down over the lough to drop their payloads on the port and industrial heartland. However unintentional it might have been, many planes overshot their original targets and managed to destroy two thirds of the domestic housing stock in Belfast, killing a thousand people in the process and injuring many more. Fire crews were emasculated by the fact that a reservoir in north Belfast was seemingly breached to prevent them drawing essential amounts of water. This was the greatest single loss of life in one evening outside London made all the worse by the fact the planes acted without any hindrance. Titus now knew the difference between allied and enemy engines, he had no cause to panic as long as he didn't suffer a direct hit and was buried in the rubble. He had a large cellar to retreat to when he heard the sirens sound out another raid and he preferred this to the clammy throng of the surface shelters which were packed to distraction. These surface shelters in many cases were modified former public lavatories and smelled to high heaven. They were often the focus of nefarious black market activity and tended to be frequented by the lowest sort of people intent on no good. Many more people simply died in their homes, which in many cases were built in terraces hard by the factory walls, which were now receiving a pounding.

Titus had seen his fair share of devastation, be it from cannon shot or incendiary, he saw how people reacted differently in wartime. They lived as normally as they could in a hazardous environment that he thought akin to living under a glass cloche which could smash at any time. War expelled the need for introspection, it made heroes out of some in action, but it also made any hard earned peace hard to live with. War was shameful and brought out the worst vices in those who sought to exploit its distraction for their own gain. War also bonded people like no other, the bombing of so many cities was returned in spades to the German people, who instead of giving in, only worked harder for their war effort. He could never get over how people tended to act differently when under duress. Not the kind of pressure induced from work or financial worry, but the kind that awoke people to the thought that this day might be their last and that they should probably live it as though it were. This war was a cloak, which adorned intrigue and opportunity. People took chances they normally wouldn't have done in peace time, crimes often went unrecorded in the black-outs. Bombed out buildings were ripe for pillage as long as they didn't collapse in on you. Those children from poorer backgrounds who were not evacuated couldn't resist joining gangs to plunder fresh bombsites during the air raids. Streets and districts that had been pulverised took on a new persona and the Police were stretched too thinly to keep the looters at bay. Bridge Street lay at one end of Joys Entry and was of no strategic importance but that didn't stop the marker flares lighting up the entries that lay around it. So many buildings had fallen within its vicinity that Bridge Street had now its own reservoir to supply the fire engines, courtesy of the river Farset which still flowed under the culverts. Titus knew the risk but still he couldn't resist unlocking his attic room as another barrage of phosphor flares fell on the city. He opened his sky light window and latched it. It was compulsively macabre viewing, landmarks in all directions were laced in gold plumes, which licked and consumed factories and churches indiscriminately. High above his head the bombers could be clearly seen forming a series of grey crucifixes in the ink canopy. They came on in perfect formation and were buffered by the flak that emitted from what looked like the peashooters below. Searchlights operated from different sites across the city, they crossed swords with one another latching on to one target which still had its bomb bay doors wide open. The Heinkel gained altitude and began to merge with the night sky until it disappeared. Others took its place in a symmetry of death, orderly and organised. The industrial areas were festooned in flame licks and black smoke. Giant gasholders spouted fumes and fury with direct hits and the cranes by the quayside seemed to buckle with the heat on their gantries. All the while there was that drone, until the last tail fin disappeared between the fume clouds that enveloped the city. When that had died away, the sirens and alarms quickly took their place.

On the morning after that particularly heavy raid Titus decided to try and make his way to the hardware store in Castle Junction. He now carried out daily routine damage inspections throughout his building. The heat from the bombings had induced fire sparks, which had drifted in the night air and settled on his upper floor windowsills. They had taken hold on the paintwork of two window frames, melting the paint and shattering some of the intricate glass panels. He measured the panels and found them to be slightly different in length. He was greeted outside by an ashen powder covering which was reminiscent of light snow but definitely the wrong colour for any Christmas card. It coated every surface and even those who he brushed passed had a sprinkling of it on their clothes. A tram had derailed at the top of the street and was abandoned before last night's bombings. Shredded curtains formed what looked like a ticker tape procession from the smashed up windows of the surrounding buildings. Mannequins from dress hire shops were naked on the pavement, their outfits taken in the night. It was as if every shop owner had the same idea to board up their premises for the duration, men in overalls with nails in their teeth hammered planks into the jagged window frames. The main avenue was pock marked at intervals by a caved in shop front with either smoke or steam and sometimes both emanating from them. Floor plans and the accoutrements of private lives were on parade, cut through evenly with armchairs and standard lamps precariously balanced. Service men and civilians formed in ragged lines were scratching at the debris and shouting for any signs of life. They removed splintered architraves and uprooted fire surrounds, but found no survivors. Fire crews and Firewatchers sat exhausted by their tenders with blackened faces which spoke silently of what they had seen overnight. Salvation Army tea urns where manned and they handed out blankets to those who needed them. At the junction a large gun emplacement was being re-supplied behind a sandbag barricade. Empty shell cases littered the road and were being gathered up by raggedy children. These brass cases would be smelted again as brass was in short supply with the war effort. Tired soldiers shared cigarettes in the drizzle and watched through their gun sights as the seagulls made rich targets over the Bank Buildings. Boy Scouts were acting as stretcher-bearers taking the dead to the grounds of the City Hall where they could be formally identified. None of this made any sense any more, the usual was a thing of the past and Titus soon forgot what he had actually left his house for. He smelled the air, traces of cordite and burning petroleum. How much more could this town take he wondered, and then he looked around again at all the activity. These people hadn't given in, if anything they were angry, but that too remained buried beneath their convictions. He had seen this before and he wanted to try and help in some way. He saw a number of Red Cross vehicles make their way in the direction of the Corn market.

He followed and soon arrived at a makeshift dressing station. An army doctor was looking at a chart outside a large tent in the centre of the square. Titus brushed passed some nurses and approached the officer.

'I was wondering if I could be of help in any way?' he asked tentatively.

The doctor was a Captain and he had a blood stained white coat over his uniform. He had just reprimanded his Corporal for taking ages in returning with morphine phials from the Mater hospital. The poor fellow looked crestfallen, forgetting his rank momentarily and bellowed that the roads were treacherous and that he needed more men to protect the lorry from profiteers who had tried to steal the morphine in the hospital car park.

'That's enough of that tone Corporal. Take the phials to the attending Staff nurse and report back to me double quick.'

Titus could sense a grudging regard between the two soldiers as they too looked exhausted.

'Who the hell are you?' the Captain asked.

'My name is Unlive sir. I have a house nearby with a large cellar that I have made presentable. If you would permit me I can take the overspill of patients you have and you can arrange nursing supervision for them.'

'What did you say your name was?'

'Unlive. Titus Unlive.'

'Damned strange name that. This cellar, is it damp?'

'No, I have used it as a dry store for many years and I can promise you there is no damp.'

'Bit odd this all the same. Are you a medical man? I can see that you are a bit too old to serve. Are you Home Guard by any chance?'

'No, I was once an apothecary, or a you might call it a chemist.'

'I see, and you say this house is not far from here?'

'Not far at all, within a ten minute walk.'

'Well no one else has offered us any space, so I don't see why not.'

The Corporal arrived back and the Captain told him to get one of the duty nurses to accompany him and Mr Unlive back to his home and check if the cellar suited purpose.

'My name is Masterson, Captain Masterson. Bloody glad to know you Mr Unloved.'

Titus laughed into himself, it was all he could do when he looked around at the organised confusion. The Corporal and the nurse walked through the ash coated streets and he listened as the soldiers gripes reached a crescendo before Unlive reminded him that he was in the presence of a lady.

'You actually live here mate?'

'Yes I do.'

'Bit bloody spooky if you ask me!'

The nurse overlooked these remarks and asked to see the cellar. Unlive led them down a flight of stairs lined by unrendered walls.

'Watch your step, these boards are old, but they have served me well. I have sufficient lighting down here and over there you will find a water closet.'

The cellar was about twenty metres in length and a man of six foot could just about manage to stand up straight within it. Importantly it had pillars supporting its ceiling, they had been reinforced over the years as a result of gradual subsidence. Ventilation was supplied by narrow grilled panes which met at street level above. The floor was tiled and well maintained and along the far wall stood a row of ornate barrels of aged oak.

'Do you make your own grog?' asked the Corporal.

'These barrels contain oil not alcohol I'm afraid. I store them for the Alhambra restaurant which operates a few streets away. They pay me a small retainer to use this space.'

'I think I've seen enough, what about you nurse?'

'Trainor, my name is Hazel Trainor,'

'Pleased to meet you Hazel.' said the Corporal.

'This will do well Mr Unlive.' she said

'Good I'm pleased, I just wanted to do my bit.'

'Then that's settled, we will push off now and return with some of the walk in casualties as soon as.'

'I will wait for your return then, let me know if there is anything else you need.' said Titus.

Nurse Trainor followed the Corporal back up the steps and onto the landing. She had calculated that there was probably enough space within to treat up to fifty patients comfortably. This wasn't much, but it would ease the congestion back at the medical tent.

Later that afternoon the cellar was decked out in trestle tables and collapsible cots that would have been better suited to camping expeditions. Gas lamps had been added for extra light and canvas sheeting had been hung for privacy to divide up the cellar space. Sawdust was sprinkled liberally on the floor to soak up any spilt blood and soon the room began to fill with medical personnel, equipment and patients. Titus kept a ledger of the names of each patient to be treated, their ailment and diagnosis. When the sirens sounded for the evening attack he had sixty-seven names on his list either waiting or being treated. He counted fifteen nurses and three doctors working in his cellar. The familiar drone above was now masked by the moans and wails of those suffering from the previous nights raid. The space seemed to shake with the impact above, but the pillars held and the doctors went about their work systematically. The electricity supply flickered then gave up entirely as the bombing took hold. Many of the younger patients began to cry with the disorientation. Titus took a gas lamp and made his way to the far end of the cellar. Beside the oak kegs there was a sideboard and he unlocked it and took out some earthenware mugs. He left the lamp on top of the sideboard and placed a mug under the tap of one of the kegs and began to pour. The noise outside was enough of a distraction for everyone so Titus drained sufficient oil into each of the five mugs until they were all full. He walked to the head of a row of cots, fifteen in length along the cellar wall. These people had been given first aid or remedial attention, they all had fear etched on their faces, they all had lost something, only to be replaced by uncertainty. They had blackened faces and fresh bandages, flesh wounds that could be patched up and memories that would leave them scarred and shattered. Titus passed a cup to the first patient and then told them to take a sip and pass it on down the line. They did so without fail, no one grabbed the cup or took more than a sip as it would have been so tempting to do. He walked slowly down each aisle and watched their reactions as he progressed. They in turn pressed it to their lips without hesitation. There in the midst of this onslaught, he saw the look he always read as akin to salvation on their faces, the colour had returned to their worried brows and they now lay or sat with composure. He repeated the dosage to the next row under the gas lamps, which now swung slowly on their pillar mountings. Masonry cracked and flaked from all surfaces, but the cellar still held intact. Tired nurses watched him without reacting as he passed the mugs down the line, hands reaching in the half-light to quench their fears. For everyone who drank was now free from fear, free to heal, free to take on whatever might come with renewed vitality and vigour. This was a shared sacrament, unspoken in the din of an air raid. A clutch of doctors watched from the sidelines, until at length the mugs were empty and Titus wiped them clean and placed them back in the sideboard for safe keeping. Overhead the maelstrom dissipated and the sinister drone melted into the ancient foundations of Titus's dwelling.

It was safe now to sleep, the sleep that had for so long been denied and kept out of reach by terror and worry. Sleep was the balm that helped ferment the oil from within. How many times had he seen this before? The oil was a form of contrition, it took away not the sin, but the hallmarks on the physical, it cleansed the body from within. He knew he could never explain this to weary physicians who would balk at any convoluted explanation. So he just did what he thought was necessary to ease their pain, using other methods.

When he thought it was sufficiently safe to do so, Titus returned upstairs and began to write in his journal. He put a tick beside the sixty-seven names, people from all parts of a stricken city, from all religions and backgrounds. A young commissioned doctor followed him upstairs and pressed on to the front door of Unlive's house. He lit a cigarette at the half open doorway and gazed at the night sky, which glowed amber in the heat from the firestorm. Titus walked over to him and they stood in silence for a moment as the city they both knew so well turned in on itself in the flames.

'I didn't think it my place to say anything back there, Mr Unlive, but what did you just do to those people?'

'I gave them back hope.'

'Hope in the form of a drink?'

'If you like, yes. I don't expect you to understand this, but by the act of sharing a cup, the sincerity it promotes also provides hope.'

'That's before I even ask you what was in those mugs you handed out!'

'You can ask of course, the answer you will hear will be as alien to you as one of Saturn's moons up there, but it will be the truth.'

'Then I will just leave it there orbiting Saturn where it belongs Mr Unlive. I saw something return to them afterwards, a kind of grace settled over the room as you moved among them. They are all asleep now for the first time, the raids were still in full swing and somehow they all began to sleep through it. I won't lie to you, at first I thought you had doped the poor critters, but then I knew you just wanted to share something of yours with them.'

'I did, I am obliged to, if you know what I mean. It's a calling. You people have worked so hard through the night, I just wanted to sustain their nerves through the darkest part of the raid.'

Morning brought with it a fresh coating of the fire dust that did it's best to conceal the rape of the City. The consecutive raids had wrought more havoc than even an enemy bomb aimer could have hoped. Resilience is no metal and certainly cannot be bent out of shape with the impact of so many tonnes of high explosive. Resilience can take many forms and like a fire it can spread too in the spirit of defiance that was tangible on the faces of those unfortunates in Belfast. A cup of tea and some hard tack biscuit was all that was on offer in the cellar that morning, but the walking wounded drained their cups and set back out to discover whether or not they still had a place to call home. It was uncertain if another raid would follow, if it had, then what then? All they knew was that they couldn't give up.

When it was felt sure that the night raiders had moved their attentions to fresh targets, the authorities wound down the cellar triage unit and slowly Titus got his space back and the lasting thanks of many. He caught himself missing all the frenetic activity, the intensity, the character it brought out under duress of those from whom others took their lead. This town was on its knees, but it wasn't bowed. Staff nurse Trainor was one of the last to leave and Titus offered to accompany her back to the field dressing station in the Corn Market. She had shown a phlegmatic determination during the raids which had impressed him. She in turn had more than once reached out for his arm to enable her to balance as they made their way across the desolate terrain. Whatever thoughts that percolated through her mind remained unspoken for awhile amid the devastation, but she felt safe with him. At length they passed through the cordons and in the relative safety she turned to him.

'Please don't take this the wrong way,' she said 'but there is something different about you, isn't there?'

'You think? What like, is it the hair, the accent?'

She knew he was joshing with her and she couldn't help but smile.

'Come away with that Mr Unlive, you know what I mean.'

'You tell me then.' he said.

'Well, throughout the raids down there, I hardly saw you sleep. It was as if you felt it your duty to watch over everybody. You never seemed tetchy and you never let your guard down, even as the cellar shook.'

'I was scared, but I'm ready for whatever comes, if it is my time. I think if you are at ease with yourself, then you can prepare for anything. I guess that I never want to die alone, when the time comes and that if it had then I would rather fall with you people.'

'That was what I was trying to get at, nothing seems to faze you and that confidence helped allay the fears of those who sheltered here.'

'So that's a compliment then?' he asked.

'Yes if you like, I have more if you care to ask me back some time.'

'You would like to come back here, to visit?'

'Do I have to spell it out for you? D A T E!'

'You want to go on a date with me?' he recoiled.

Staff nurse Trainor tugged on her cape as she laughed.

'Why the hell not, life's too short!' he said ironically. When do you have a night off this week?' he asked.

'I'm due some time off on Thursday night is that okay? she asked.

'Thursday, say 7pm, I could pick you up outside the Mater?'

'Perfect, we could eat at yours and then go to the picture house. I still haven't seen Casablanca yet, have you?'

'Erh no.' he replied awkwardly.

Titus certainly hadn't seen Casablanca, in fact he hadn't seen any moving picture since their inception. He had shunned invention to help cultivate his remoteness. He had never learnt to drive, he lived without a telephone, preferring correspondence and only recently had he converted the house from gas to electricity. This was the paradox of his long existence. He could have been at the forefront of innovation, after all he had plenty of time to adapt, but conversely he couldn't be seen to influence change. If you can't alter, tinker, modify, no matter what the age, then you soon get frustrated and turn your back on things. He had done just that. He put it down to his sedentary lifestyle without a companion to share it with. For what use was he to a woman? He was cruel to himself in his inability to please one. Over time he had rebuffed advances from any quarter with a cold politeness. Advances came and went over many lifetimes, Titus was single and of means and not unattractive. His social life was minimal and he derived some solace in not being exposed to the petty ruminations of society. It did mark him out as a loner, but he didn't mind this at all. Those that mocked, would over time dwindle, the salons and drawing rooms that once echoed with their idle gossip would fall into neglect and become rooms to withdraw from as the house was slowly shut up to visitors. Yet here he was, he had found himself saying yes to a date with Hazel Trainor, to entertaining her in his home no less. He had said yes with such an easy reliance that had only compounded the grains of attraction that he was steadily gathering for her. He walked away from her, forgetful of the angst that had propelled his protective instincts. He walked away from her with a spring in his step that he hadn't felt since consuming the oil for the first time. He had a warm glow in his heart and he didn't quite know what to do about it. It was only a date, but it had come from her mouth, natural and well intentioned with wit to match his reticence, taking things to another level. What the hell was he going to cook for her? He decided to visit Mullans Bookshop in Donegall Place on the way home to try and pick up some ideas. Mercifully Mullans was untouched by the bombing and a defiant hand written sign was pinned to the window stating business as usual. Titus was in his element, his real vice was literature and he embellished his home with first editions. His library was his bolthole, but within it there was little on the art of entertaining or cuisine for that matter.

Mullans was his forgetting place; it was a trustworthy armoire as a respite from the streetscape. The staff knew him well, his penchants having been finely honed in the intervening centuries. His enthusiasm for knowledge acted as a counter balance to his reluctance to change. Mullans had become a mainstay in a pattern that revolved around daily visits to Brands and Normans for morning coffee and the now heavily rationed food parcels wrapped in string and brown paper from Sawyers delicatessen. He raised a few eyebrows as he climbed the spiral staircase to the non-fiction department. The cookery section was new territory, but the choice was ample and he took advantage of a shabby leather chair as he leafed through some books that he thought might be of help. He settled for a collection of articles by an English Francophile called Elizabeth David. She was young and exuberant and her enthusiasm poured off the collection of articles she had written from abroad. He connected with her style. He smiled into himself as she conjured new themes on the cuisine of his younger days when his family lived in relative peace in La Rochelle on the Biscay coast. He could cook this he thought, sure the ingredients might be sparse, but even he could muster up a coq au vin. At length he returned downstairs to the familiar hunting grounds of classic fiction and poetry. He couldn't resist a frayed and battered edition of Vasari's 'Lives of the Great Artists', so he took the David and Vasari to the bookseller at the front desk.

'Good morning Mr Unlive, I didn't see you come in,' said Godfrey.

Titus nodded and handed the books over to be wrapped in cord.

'Elisabeth David's articles on French cuisine? This is a departure for you.'

'Yes Godfrey I don't quite know how I got this far without a cookery book to show for it.'

'Not too many meals with dried egg and desiccated milk amongst those I imagine.' Godfrey demurred.

'This war won't last forever Godfrey and I can throw in other ingredients. French cookery is very adaptable, some of these are peasant recipes and aren't difficult or contrived.'

'If I didn't know better I would hazard that you are trying to impress someone with your cookery skills.'

'Thank you Godfrey, I love our little chats, you bring such insight into my otherwise opaque existence.'

Godfrey hands over Titus's change and Unlive bids farewell as the bell in the doorframe echoes his departure.

'Where did you learn to cook like that?' asked Hazel.

'I had help I must admit, I'm glad you liked it.'

'It was sublime, was there some kind of marinade?'

'I steeped the chicken overnight in fortified wine with orange peel and cinnamon.'

'It melted off the bone, I haven't eaten so well since the war began.'

'Let me clear your plates away.' he said.

'Your dinner ware is so finite, I didn't know which knife to use.'

'I so rarely have guests so I had quite forgotten how to set a table. These plates are Sevres porcelain, a favourite of the Emperor Napoleon, they have his bumblebee motif at the centre. Reproduction of course! The crystal came from a grateful client, I think it ages well even though it is quite heavy to lift.'

'The wine is unlike anything I have ever tasted.' she said.

Hazel drained her glass and rose to help him clear away the plates. She asked for the direction to the toilet and disappeared down the hall. When she returned Titus has served up a cold compote with some blancmange on two dessert plates.

'That looks good.' A voice, not Hazel's, comes out of the shadows. Hazel stands with her arms folded over a high chair back as the figure emerges from behind her.

'What have we here?' He stood behind her for a moment and offered his hand to her mouth suggestively. She in turn bit down hard on his palm while staring straight through Titus, the intruder reeled from the bite and pulled on her long hair as he pushed her aside. Titus could make him out now, his pinched looks with beady eyes, partly hidden under a flat cap.

'Real cosy here innit pal? Just you snuggling up to my girl after a feed.'

Hazel moved closer to him as she heard him mention her, she licked his unshaven face and laughed in Titus's direction.

'You let this person into my house? You actually consort with this type?'

'Consort is one way of putting it.' she sniggered. 'He's my fella, a bit rough round the edges, but I can iron him out.'

'Spare me the details, both of you. Get out now before this gets ugly.'

'The only thing ugly here is your wizened face, you dirty oul git.'

Titus was still sitting across from them when the intruder lunged at him and they both toppled over the chair and struggled with each other on the floor. Hazel stuck a finger into the compote and licked it, defiantly detached, certain of the outcome. Her fella was strong and soon had Titus choking with his grasp.

'You thought you could sweet talk your way into my girl's arms. Do you like playing doctors and nurses, because I'm going to give you an injury you posh gobshite!'

Titus was losing. He could feel the blood draining from him as the pressure on his neck grew ever stronger. He pulled at the tablecloth and the dinnerware collapsed around them sending splinters across the polished floorboards. This distracted his assailant long enough for him to be able to smack his head with a blunt fist thereby releasing his attackers grip. Hazel stepped over them both and released Titus from any consciousness by kicking him in the side of his head, hard enough for blood to emerge from his ear.

'My wee girl.' said the intruder.

She helped him to his feet and he wiped his bloody mouth with a well used handkerchief. He perched on the edge of the dining table, catching his breath and grabbed Hazel. Their adrenalin matched so he spread her legs open, hitching up her skirt, he seized upon her underwear before roughly mounting her.

'Some people never learn,' she uttered before being overcome by his ardour.

Hazel's relationship with Michael Furey had got off to a very unauspicious start some three years earlier, when as a ward nurse she had caught him rifling through the secure medicine cabinets in the small hours of the morning at the Mater hospital. Furey was searching for anything he could fence on the black market and saw Hazel as collateral damage. He roughed her up enough to deter her from crying out for help. She was infuriated by her own weakness to defend herself from his grasp as he gagged her and dragged her back into the night office at the end of the ward. Michael Furey then indulged himself with her, ploughing a rabid furrow along the folds of her starched uniform. Hazel struggled, scoring his cheek superficially with her nails before he took her wrists away behind her head and coldly he unravelled her. His wound bled on her face and it dripped onto her gag as he tied her wrists together. Furey then unscrewed the bulb in her desk lamp and in her riotous mind she found herself alive to his unkempt hands groping all over her and the musk that exuded from under his frayed shirt collar. Furey held her throat tight enough to scare, loose enough to invite a thrill of anxiety that now shot freely through her every cell. She had struggled with him and now she writhed with him as they connected on the cold linoleum. He pushed her face away before licking her ear, his warm saliva began to drip slowly down the side of her face which was now pressed tight against the waste paper basket and the filing cabinet. They flayed on the office floor and her tender fingers soon slipped free from the knot he had tied only to find herself pulling on the belt around his waist to reveal his firm buttocks. She pressed them into her ever tighter until they both came in a frenzy in the darkness.

Hazel Trainor 24, came from Twaddell Avenue, she had attended an all girl convent school and had never met anyone quite like Michael Furey before. She was only covering for a friend as a favour that evening and might never have apprehended him, but she had and it changed her as a result. She raised herself off the floor and sat by the desk. Light from the streetlamps outside highlighted the gash she had made on Furey's face. She reached for the bulb and screwed it back into the light fitting. Furey remained on the floor and she instinctively opened a dressing and poured disinfectant on it before applying it to his face. He didn't flinch and sat straight ahead as she secured the dressing to his cheek, his jacket pockets bulged with the stolen phials of morphine and other bottles he had taken from the medicine cabinet. Without speaking he rose and stroked her face with his coarse hands. He leant down and kissed her head. Hazel had been accosted by a thief on the ward, she had been tied up against her will and then assaulted. She had then succumbed to a passion that had hitherto never manifested itself, consuming any propriety before devouring her in fit of fearsome sex. Hazel was now involved and found herself willing to be so. Michael Furey had until now only ever formed loose attachments with women, being unable to suffer what he saw as the constraints they demanded on his freedom. He was never stifled by morality, always seeking new and underhand ways to find the enrichment that always seemed to be just around the corner. It never occurred to him that he might form a relationship with this nurse who would never normally have looked twice at him in the street. His background on the lower Falls had taught him from an early age to take what he could and bugger the consequences. She was an obstacle and he had dealt with her, he had to shut her up and in the process he had grappled with her. Her defence had only fuelled his resolve, he wasn't going to get caught, but as they fought he was overtaken by something primeval that boiled over into desire. He knew he was a low life thug with no good intent, he was malicious even, but as his hands strayed over her uniform, he swore he felt a mutual passion emerge from deep within her at the same time.

Titus had been left for dead. Hazel kept watch as Michael Furey took free reign of no.13. He started in the attic space, which was floored and had remained unoccupied for some time. He toppled over tea chests and rummaged through their contents. Furey in his ignorance neglected to put any value to the pair of miniature Pieter de Hooch oil paintings that Unlive had been given as a token of esteem by the Bulmer family. Instead Furey was taken by the seventeenth century jewellery box that had belonged to Titus's mother. He opened the box and pocketed the clasp that was dated 1665 within. It was one of the last tokens given to his mother on her wedding anniversary. Furey began walking through the rooms searching for anything he might fence on. He tore back the dust covers as he went, kicking open doors and shoving goblets and vases into an old coal sack which he slung over his back. Hazel waited quietly below, she had poured more of the delicious wine Titus had served her earlier in the evening. She could here her fella's excitable steps as he emerged onto different landings with the clanking sack at his shoulder. Above this, if she cared to listen, she might have heard the laboured breaths coming from Titus. Her kick to the side of his head had knocked him out and fractured the cartilage in his right ear. She missed giving him cranial damage, but the splinters had fractured his eardrum and it was haemorrhaging. Hazel was oblivious to all this, she made no diagnosis and hadn't gone near his prone body since delivering the blow. She sat at the dining table, which was now scored from the gyration of her lover's belt. She looked through the cut glass she had been drinking from as it made patterns onto the wall. These walls were adorned with prints and hangings that had been gathered over time by Titus to comfort his longevity. The room had two windows and these were now shuttered, but she could still feel a draft coming from them.

The fire which Titus had set to welcome her, was now dying back in the grate. It was probably a good thing that Titus was unaware of her presence as he would not have been capable of fathoming her baseness. Hazel Trainor had kept her job at the Mater, she had been commended even for her bravery against an assailant. She in turn was now Furey's accomplice, turning a blind eye just often enough at the hospital to his activities so as not to arouse too much suspicion. It was her that tipped Michael off about a soft target who had surrounded himself with trinkets and resalable items on the black market. Furey had encouraged her to befriend this character and gain his trust. Hazel was the plausible front for his scurrilous activities, she had unbolted the door that evening as she had pretended to use Titus's toilet. She had seen Furey's methods, his greedy inclinations, which she thought she had tempered with her own brand of cold determination from whence she was unable to say where it came. She drained her glass and threw it at a wall hanging that somehow displeased her, at that moment Michael returned to the dining room. He had seen enough.

'Hang on a minute,' she said 'the cellar!'

'Lead on darlin.' he said.

Hazel knew the way well. She grabbed Michael's hand and led him across the hallway to the door beneath the main staircase. She flicked the switch above the doorknob and it lit their way down to the cellar space.

Michael shook his head at so much free space and as his eyes adjusted to the dark shadows until he could make out the barrels in the corner.

'Does this bloke make his own homebrew then or what?'

'I wanted to show you this darling, I saw him ration it out to the patients we had down here during the air raids the other night.' she said

'So is it some kind of medicine then?' he asked.

'Whatever it is it fortified those people, it must be some kind of relaxant, it made them all tranquil and dozy even.'

'This I have got to try. Do you see any mugs down here at all?'

'He kept some beakers in that sideboard from what I remember, try opening one of those cupboard doors.'

Michael reached in and grabbed one of the mugs. He smiled at Hazel and made the money gesture with his fingers. She sidled up to him as he bent the handle on the tap of one of the kegs and poured out the golden liquid.

'No head on this. Pity,' he quipped.

'It doesn't need to have a head, try it.' she said.

Michael put the mug to his lips and drank in the Kingsevil. He hadn't tasted anything like it before and at first he thought he might gag with the liquid intensity mixed with the oils pungent unfamiliarity. He found he liked it and took even greater gulps. Hazel laughed as it began to spill over his unshaven skin and down his front. He wiped his mouth with his jacket sleeve and grabbed another mug for her.

'Here darlin' you try this stuff, its nectar all right.' he slurred.

Hazel could see the pleasure Michael derived from drinking nearly the whole measure he had poured. She grabbed her mug and drank it down, mindless of how much had spilt over her dress. She sensed a subtle nuance within the mug that momentarily led her to believe that the wine she had been drinking earlier might have contained some of its essence. No matter she bargained, this was the stuff that had made people rest easy during an air raid, it must have some peculiar qualities to be able to relax anybody during such duress. They quenched more and drew up a stool upon which she sat on his lap as he kissed her between gulps. After the first mug they had lost track of time, the oil was numbing the senses and lolling the two of them. They soon had drunk more than it was safe to do so and they both flailed lazily on the cellar floor, until they fell asleep.

Titus was conscious of the blood congealing in his ear. The draft coming through the floorboards had started to dry the blood around his wound. He at first could only lie there on his dining room floor, until his eyes regained their symmetry allowing him to focus on one feature at a time.

The shards of porcelain plate that encircled his broken frame, the sparkle of crushed crystal that lay just feet from him. The fine art that now left only their shadows on the wallpaper, broken frames and rolled up canvases tossed into the grate for warmth. He felt anger and was glad of it as it told him he was still able to think. He felt two sharp pains in his side and deduced that he had broken some ribs in his fight with the attacker. His hair had matted with sweat convexly narrowing his outlook. He was relieved to be able to adjust his hair with his right hand. He reached out for the chair leg. His head was groggy and he laboured over raising it level with the chair seat. He saw the scratched veneer on the dining room table and this gave him the impetus to raise himself fully. The dining room door was ajar and light came flooding in from the hallway. Titus stood for a moment holding his side and craning his matted head slowly around the room, which had been of so much comfort to him for so long.

He crushed shards inadvertently under foot as he felt strong enough to walk over to the mahogany drinks cabinet. The drinks tray was half stocked above and in the cupboard below he reached for a flagon of the Kingsevil oil. He knew what his body required and he poured the equivalent amount into a glass of sack. He knocked it back sharply and poured another. The restitution it provided warmed his body sufficiently giving him the strength to plough on through the house. He now stood in the hallway and saw the crude sack that had been dumped there full of his possessions garnered over many lifetimes. The anger he now felt blocked out any rationale he had ever learnt. He gathered up his mother's jewellery box and prized it open. The clasp was intact within and he sighed momentarily at the anguish of ever being parted from it. He walked down the hallway to the front door, which Michael had closed, but not bolted. He opened the door and walked a few paces down the alleyway, passed the delivery trap door within the walkway until he could see the section of iron grilles that projected from his basement at street level. Within he could see the dimly lit cellar and just make out the outline of two figures slumped upon the floor. He went back inside with the knowledge that the pair who attacked him wouldn't be awake to his intentions. Titus made his way down the cellar steps, his chest now ached numbly thanks to the amount of oil he had drunk. Flinging open the coalhole door, he reached inside for some dirty sacks and draped then under the grilles at street level. He was certain that he would not be seen now and any noise he created would be muffled by the thickness of the cellar walls. He approached the coalhole opening and was about to slam it shut when he saw the lengthy shovel used on delivery days. He grabbed the shovel and leaned on it as his assailants snored on the cellar floor. Titus wondered how much they had drunk. Wondering only invited a chink of pity into his heart, a pathetic glimmer soon subdued by the desecration and abuse he had undergone. Still holding the shovel he approached the pair, Hazel's best dress somewhat the worse for a rolling about on a dusty cellar floor. Furey lay face down by her side, his breathing steady, enviable even Titus thought in that Furey had no conscious awareness of what he had done and what he was about to befall. Titus used the shovel as balance with one arm, sliding down it as gently as his ribs would let him.

He grabbed a clump of Michael Fureys hair raising his head over Hazel. Furey moaned at the sudden pain in his head and opened his drowsy eyelids.

'Did you think to leave me up there to die? Did you think me dead already? Did you even care to check whether or not I still breathed?'

Michael Furey interrupted from the sleep of the just now awoke fully to the reality of the unjust. Titus let go of his greasy hair and Michael's face slumped over Hazel's chest. How appropriate Titus thought, that she should catch his fall for one last time. Furey tried to gather in his surroundings, but was unable to move. Titus rose using the shaft for leverage.

'You didn't think twice about entering my house uninvited. Your friend here was invited and she both duped and humiliated me by letting you in. Your lover whose name I am too disgusted to utter released your contagion into the place where I feel safest.'

Furey tried again to move and found his shoulder being imprinted by the heel of Titus's shoe. He gave up and pressed his face into Hazel's chest in the hope the pressure might revive her. She slept on unaware of the one sided conversation. Titus felt confident enough to release his shoe and walk around and face Furey.

'How very rude of me, we haven't even been introduced, my name is Titus Unlive and yours is? Let me guess, oh that's right I've got it now, your name is thuggish lout who left me for dead. Pleased to meet you I'm sure. You see your name doesn't matter anymore, you gave it up with all other privileges when you entered my house. You don't matter anymore, not that you ever did, as you are about to be executed by a man who in the eyes of the law is already dead.'

Michael could only listen, he couldn't feel his legs as the oil had done its job, his heartbeat was subdued but his mind was racing. How did this guy survive the beating he had given him? As well as Hazel's coup de grace to the head. Hazel, he thought, please wake up, maybe Unlive might show some grain of sentiment to her.

'You think she might stop what I am about to perform on you. Your death is a perfunctory task, a necessity, it matters not to the dogs in the street or any other living thing what we do down here this day.'

With these words still ringing in his ears, Furey is dragged back by his wrists over to the coalhole doorway. He fancies momentarily that Unlive is stronger than he looks, desperately trying to negate the fact that he was bested by a much older man. Control was always Michael Furey's middle name. A small time thief with a skulking flare to maximise the misfortune of others. He didn't just rob from his own, he rubbed it in by flaunting it in the pubs they drank in. He mistook infatuation for affection and corrupted any woman he came in contact with blaming it when drunk on the neglect of his parents. Yes, introspection had always been in short supply until his shoe leather began to scrape the flagstones before being unceremoniously draped at the base of the coal stack.

'Have you anything you would like to say before you leave this earth?' Titus asked without emotion. Michael Furey, rotten to the core, looked over at Hazel one last time.

'For Christ's sake have a little pity man!' he pleaded.

Hazel was still out cold, but Michael continued to focus on her.

'Pity unlike coal is in short supply down here.' Unlive said dryly.

Titus raised the shovel until its shadow met with Furey's head and then he arched it and swung it using momentum to harness the blade. It severed an artery, ushering a reflex action from Furey. The jettison paralysed him with fear as Unlive carried through his task snapping through bone and sinew with ease. Michael Furey, housebreaker, philanderer, a low life guttersnipe who wouldn't be missed, now lay unblinking through a severed head in the coal dust.

Titus nudged the coal stack with the shovel, it came away and deluged the stricken remains until it lay buried under ten feet of coal. He would worry about the body in the spring, but only if the smell became unbearable. He placed the shovel at an angle in the coal as some kind of perverse headstone and closed the door. He went into the adjoining lavatory, it had been well stocked since the time of the triage unit. He washed his hands thoroughly and then blew the excess coal dust from his nostrils. He looked at himself for a moment in the mirror and noticed Hazel move from where she had lain for so long. Titus walked over to her. She was unable to protest as he bent her neck back and unfastened the necklace Furey had stolen from one of the upstairs rooms. He took out her earrings which were her own. He took off her own watch, her own bracelet and her shoes. All Hazel could do was watch passively as he pulled off the black market nylons Furey had bought her. He took off her jacket and began making tears in her dress, not too many, just enough to terrify her. Titus now winced as he tried to lift her, his broken ribs moaned their disapproval. He got her arm over his shoulder and was relieved that she appeared to be taking some of the weight herself. They faltered in the stairway and Titus caught her drooling as she stared right through him, still under the influence of the Kingsevil oil. She moaned in his ear, undecipherable truths, best kept to herself he thought. In the hallway he set her down on a chair beside the coal sack full of his stolen goods. Hazel looked over the contents and appeared to try and mouth something to him. He now looked at his watch, 3.15am. How long had he been unconscious for? He knew that this woman had wanted him dead and he most certainly would have been but for the oil. Titus now put on his greatcoat and was confident Hazel wasn't going anywhere. He locked her in and proceeded down the entry to the junction with High Street. The sizzling aftermath that had prevailed for days opened up before him in the toothless vista of blown out shop fronts and disjointed gable walls that reared up in the darkness. Bridge Street was deserted, the black out was in force and the streets were empty. He retraced his steps back to no. 13.

Hazel lay slumped in the chair, the sack had fallen over, but otherwise nothing had altered. He emptied the coal sack and then took Hazels stockings and tied her wrists with one pair and her feet with the other. She made to scream and he bunged her handkerchief in her mouth to keep her quiet. He now stood over her in the hallway.

'Look what you have turned me into. I opened myself up to you. Let you see a measure of my life and hoped that you would do the same for me. How foolish I was to believe in you, and you all that time planned and connived to rob me and then callously cancel out my life like tallow in the wind. You reaffirm my belief in the corruption of the spirit, you with the outward symbols of care, which you wear as a nurse on a daily basis. I am tempted to keep you alive as a reminder of how close I came to danger. But then I would be admitting that I was as corrupted as you.'

Titus had weighed the consequences, he could distance himself from the crime he was about to commit. If he let her go, what then? Would she keep her mouth shut? He doubted it. The scrutiny he would suffer as a result of any testimony from her, it wasn't worth the upheaval. Furey had perverted her mind and she in turn had tried to kill him, only to leave Titus as perverted as herself. Unlive knew one thing, time really was on his side. Any investigation would take into account his unselfish purveyance of the cellar for medical care. The crime he was about to commit was too grisly, too unrelated to the character of the man who lived at no.13. He bundled Hazel into the coal sack and she countered by pressing her bound feet into his neck with vice like desperation.

He punched her outline in the sack and she finally relented. Titus made a sweaty guilt laden shape as he struggled to carry her back down the alleyway to the fire tender reservoir at the junction of Bridge Street. Once sure he wasn't be observed he stacked loose masonry into the sack, she moaned as he tied its end and very awkwardly rolled the coal sack towards the incline into the reservoir. It sank without trace in only fifteen feet of murky water. Titus slumped back exhausted. He could hear the bubbles burst on the surface, then fade away. How long would it be before she was discovered? He could worry about that when he got home. He waited for a decent interval to pass and then made his way back to Joys Entry using the shadows as cover.

He was alone again amid the desecration of his home, alone and yet consumed by the twin companions of resentment and regret. He could add guilt to that list later, but for now regret would suffice. He regretted ever meeting her, offering his cellar to the medical team, letting daylight into his heart. His actions fell as dominoes towards the crimes he was cornered to commit. Perhaps he had been alive too long? He dwelled on the luxury of that negative thought until at length necessity took its place.

It was grief in reverse that spurred him. Annoyance with himself that he had been so vulnerable and the only remedy he was familiar with was toil. He could French polish the dining room table. The belt marks would only haunt him at meal times if he didn't. The wall hangings were on their last legs anyway they had taken the brunt of Hazel's anger and were coated in fortified wine. He would burn the broken picture frames and roll up their parched canvases for another era. The crystal was irreplaceable, but he saw no need to try as he would soon shut up that part of the house anyway. He replaced the items that had been unceremoniously dumped into the sack by Furey. He dusted around the cabinets in each of the rooms that had been violated, brushing the floors and shaking the mats. They were each locked in turn as he retreated downstairs, looking carefully at each section for any signs of upheaval. This was something he should have done years ago, what need had he for so much space anyway? He eventually sat on the bottom step in the cellar, below the two core wire attached to a bare light bulb that had started to sway in time with his movement down the steps. The coalhole door, firmly shut was yards away. Not today he thought, in the confusion brought about by this war, the search for Michael Furey would soon be overshadowed by the disappearance of Hazel Trainor and in time even that would be clouded out by so many other things. Time was his only real companion.

2011

When it was deemed safe to do so, the American contingent decanted from the Excelsior hotel suite that had been their base for the last two months. Thomond was strong enough to travel and Archie, his doctor relented and they both went on a pilgrimage to Limerick to see the famine tower on the bridge over the river Shannon. While in Ireland Thomond decided to parcel out much of the land purchases his company had made to charitable housing trusts or even selling the land back at reasonable prices to their original owners. To that end he had gained the board's agreement to set up an Irish department. Babbage Pharmaceuticals would operate in Europe from a base in Limerick. It had a rich well of talented individuals to draw upon. Thomond personally asked Will Donaghoe to head up the Public Relations department offering a generous relocation package to which Will nearly bit his hand off on being asked. Gemma would be a different matter and he sugared the pill by asking her to marry him. Gemma didn't hesitate and they both took great delight in handing in their notices.

Gordon McAnoy never went back into real estate. He took long term sick leave and then decided to take a course in Theology with a view to becoming a member of the Benedictine Order. He thought those long hours could be better used in the service of a higher calling. In later years he wished he could thank Sally Donnelly personally for intervening that night, robbing the office and in so doing, putting him on the road to Damascus.

Sally Donnelly never got the chance to meet Gordon again. He/She had a successful gender reassignment operation and settled in the diamond district of Antwerp. Her skills as a locksmith were much sought after by the Jewish elite and she could charge through the roof. This role briefly transformed her social status and enabled her to buy her own barge as a dream home. Sally moved in much vaunted circles by night by way of her rich contacts. Never one to hold back, she let slip her credentials to a gang of jewel thieves who had infiltrated a charity soirée. They were intent on gaining the aid of an insider whom they could blackmail. Sally fitted the bill and she was groomed by one of the gang who pretended to fall in love with her. After a botched heist in which Sally was too drunk to remember the safe combination, a gang member shot her in retaliation, fatally injuring her. She was buried without ceremony on the fringes of the Jewish cemetery in Antwerp. One of the few mourners was Blanche Orton.

Blanche Orton had followed Sally to the continent. Blanche harnessed his linguistic skills and found work as a nightclub compere in the Reeperbahn St Pauli district of Hamburg. Blanche took no prisoners with his bullet point delivery which went down well with the polyglot clientele within the red light area. The late nights suited him, the shadows and the grease paint, the decadence and the search for Mr Right. Herr Recht never quite seemed to be in the audience on a nightly basis and Orton vented his spleen between the acts with years of pent up frustration. Orton had found his niche, he re-established a new cabal based on the formative years at Quell Dommage. It was while forming this group he came back in contact with poor Sally on Twitter.

Jodi Penn parted company with Richelieu-Mazarin and applied to enrol with New York's finest NYPD. She entered the Detective fast track scheme and found she was able to express herself better than at any other time in her life. Jodi left home in Hackensack and took rooms in the Tribeca district, which thanks to Robert Di Niro had transformed itself into the cultural hub of the city. Jodi immersed herself in her chosen profession and soon opened up to romance in the guise of a drug squad lieutenant who impressed her with his own cool detachment. She had kept the feminine qualities she had both prized and flaunted and channelled them through the steely confidence her job gave her.

Sandra Morton took a redundancy package from Lydon & Dye. She decided to sell stuff for a living on ebay thus allowing her more time to devote to the one thing she really loved more than 80's music. Her dogs. Sandra still sent Will Donaghoe a CD of Spandau Ballet amongst others every Christmas and she was quick to see the irony in that he would never play them. She had caught on to her limitations and she was comfortable with them.

Titus Unlive wasn't going anywhere. Joys Entry was his dominion and he now had allies in the form of Verily Blandon amongst others who had blocked the path to change so vigorously on his behalf. If you live long enough, he laughed into himself. Who would have thought that his home would have merited so much attention as to be listed and therefore protected from development. Titus Unlive's home was resonant with the upheaval that befalls a struggling city. A city with more than its fair share of problems, some of which Titus had done his best to dilute. A home leaves an imprint through the soundings of those who once occupied it he thought. His imprint had moulded the space he had occupied continuously for over 200 years. He never filled those rooms with children or laughter, but he had preserved the integrity of the house even as he withdrew from the rooms he no longer used. The seasons forced his hand at first and he rattled about more often than not on the ground floor, leaving the upper storeys with their treasure trove of memories mothballed but intact. He liked it that way, when the urge would take him to revisit a memory of his parents, he could carefully unwrap fading embroidery his mother had spent long hours damaging her eyes to create. Or hold his father's spectacles, so brittle in the case within with his name etched in relief. Their faces had become faint to him with no image to help his recollection, only a fading outline or a gesture to direct him back to how they once looked. Just as the windowpanes had become mottled with the age, obscuring his outlook, so he had developed a cataract of his own in his mind to blot out the things that often haunted his waking moments. For every action, a reaction he thought. No matter what he had done in the past, he had acted out of protection for the oil, forever in his trust. The oil was his link with his past, it saved his life and his own skilful perseverance brought it safely through time, helping others in a way that never formed any pattern or regularity. It was up to him how he lived this eternal life, he had educated himself to be abstemious, withdrawn even, but he saw this as a necessity to the preservation of the Kingsevil. His dealings with Will Donaghoe had taught him to trust his instincts again after the carnage wrought by his falling for Hazel Trainor. He was still human after all and as vulnerable as the next man. He had the business to distract him, to which end he would offer Dominic a share to cement his role and to thank him for his loyalty. He had something else that we can never be sure of, a future, laid out before him. A vast expanse crammed into those four walls of limitless time. Time to mend, adapt, heal and create, time for him to come to terms with the man he was forever becoming.